DEATH WORE FINS

DEATH | Wore Fins

by DALE CLARK

WILDSIDE PRESS

Death Wore Fins

Published by Wildside Press LLC
www.wildsidepress.com

DEATH WORE FINS

ONE

DON DIEGO on the tourist guidance marker gestured ahead with Castilian courtesy: "Mt. Soledad."

I snapped the Leica at him and drove on up between oleanders and tulip trees and the power-clipped lawns of substantial homes. The going grew steeper, the pavement twisted, and the landscape turned to native brush dotted with estates on all possible building sites. Then it was just brush and the road hugging the canyon rim, climbing to where the millionaires lived.

Halfway up, a girl had swung out and parked on one of the curves. Her car was one of those jewel-case pink-and-cream convertibles, with fishtail fenders housing constellations of stop, directional, and backing lights. She stood at the front end, bareheaded, sticking out a sun-tanned arm, a piece of metal flashing in her wigwagging hand.

I lost momentum reluctantly. I was driving a Chevie wagon, repainted barn red, with Minnesota plates and a windshield "Press" sticker, and an air-mattress bed on the floor. Back home, I used this bus for fishing and duck-shooting week ends; it really pulled in snow and mud. But the Mt. Soledad road climbs from sea level to almost a thousand feet in less than a mile, and the rebuilt engine sounded like glassware going through the kitchen-sink disposal.

I braked the transportation almost alongside the convertible and sat there, holding the pedal down hard. The hand brake works, but it's hard to unjimmy it.

I had expected *she'd* step over—after all, she was the one flagging down traffic. But she didn't move an inch, just threw me a look from the front end of her car, and a funny look at that—sort of haughty and defiant. Around this enigmatic expression the wind was whipping strands of hair. She was brunette—make that *brown-ette*, kind of a toast brown.

The object in her hand proved to be a screwdriver, and from the way she gripped it, I got the idea she was on the defensive—the feeling she was sizing me up warily. I wondered what could ail her.

"Something wrong?" I hollered.

The girl used her screwdriver in a stabbing, annoyed gesture. "Can't you see I'm stuck?"

She was of the spoiled and petulant rich, I saw that right away. A haughty heiress queening it over the common herd. It's a brand of femininity I'd often seen portrayed on television, but to tell the truth I never believed it existed in actual life.

7

New experience beckoned, however, offering material for the canvas-bound notebook I always carry in the glove compartment— *The Journal of Kenneth Svederup*—so I hand-shifted and powered ahead in low gear for a couple of car lengths. I dropped a front tire into the cobblestoned gutter, cramped the wheel, shifted into reverse, and set the hand brake.

Then I sat still and thought twice. After all, I wasn't so eager to rush and rescue the stranded Social Registerite.

I had on a tropical suit, tailored of "imported Italian pure silk," as the Minneapolis store ad said. It wasn't tailored to measure —that would have been an extravagance, since I stand 6-1 and weigh 165 and anything that looks good on a clothes hanger fits me okay. Still, I felt no urge to peel the "luxuriously styled, faultlessly draped" coat and roll the sleeves of my $10.50 fine Danish gingham shirt all in order to tackle some blue-blooded beauty's battery cable or fuel line.

Any other time, maybe, but today I had a date to see H. H. Crossway—or to be seen by him—and after traveling fifteen hundred miles for the interview, I'd as lief not arrive in wrinkles and with motor grease under the fingernails.

There were those houses on the way up. The girl could walk to a phone in five minutes and have a tow car on the scene in ten.

"Oh, sure, take your time, you scopophiliac," said she. It was under her breath, but the wind blew from her to me.

What in hell was a scopophiliac? Even Miss Florrie Schultz in the public library back home didn't use words that long.

I hinged open the wagon's door and got out and walked back toward the girl. She still hadn't made any move and didn't now even so much as face around in my direction. So I followed the TV scripts and demonstrated she wasn't necessarily so overwhelmingly interesting to me, either.

In a leisurely fashion, I paused and contemplated the view. It was spectacular. The canyon at my feet trenched away deeply down the hillside, with the slopes of dry, desert-looking brush fanning out and framing an eagle's-eye glimpse of La Jolla, California. I could pick out the world-famed landmarks: The Bishop's School dome gleaming over the eucalyptus and palm trees, the cliff-sheltered swimming cove, the Surf and Racquet Club, the Scripps Institute of Oceanography pier sticking out from the salt-frothed shore line.

I could identify these details from the back number *National Geographic* article and the *Holiday* piece Florrie Schultz had dug out of the library file room. What is the sense of going someplace to learn what you could have found out at home? The smart deal is to know the usual tourist lore and go on from there.

I'd conned the color-plate illustrations, even to memorizing the pictured faces and matching them with the captioned names. I'd stuffed my mind with data on the Clinic, the Art Center, the Summer Playhouse, and the thirty-five resident millionaires. H. H. Crossway was one of the thirty-five, and not the low man on the local financial tote board.

I decided to tell the girl I would do the telephoning for the tow car.

"Getting an eyeful?" said she, in what might be described as a polite, or U-turned, snarl. Or in non-U, she suddenly sounded plain crying-out mad.

I quit moonily regarding the picturesque village and instead looked at her. I hadn't before, per script.

I had missed a lot. She stood there up tight against her car's front bumper grill, her skirt hiked up over the knee of the leg I could see best, the other, inner leg showing as much above that knee as below it. The pulled-tight skirt did a contour hug of her thighs and buttocks, went on up from there, and was swallowed inside the convertible's hood.

I would really have liked to take the Leica from the wagon and grab a snap for the record. Naturally, though, I didn't.

Naturally, I voiced the uppermost question in my mind; "What happened?" I asked.

"The horn jammed," she explained shortly—too shortly to explain much.

"Yuh?" I said.

"It jammed and kept on blasting like all bedlam. So I stopped and went under the hood"—she brandished the screwdriver—"to disconnect it. And just as I reached and slammed down the hood, along came a swirl of wind that blew up my darned dress."

"You couldn't raise the hood again?"

"No, it has to be released at the dash panel."

I began to understand that her petulance originated in acute embarrassment.

She's been had by a freak accident that possessed its ludicrous side just because it *was* freakish. I could see she felt more or less ridiculous, and it bothered her more than putting on the leg show. After all, she had nothing to blush for in the leg department.

"You got bear-trapped by modern technology," I remarked consolingly. "Let's face it, ours is a press-the-button age, and sometimes the button can't be reached or is out of order for reasons beyond the individual's control."

"It's a thought."

"For instance," I said, "with my old wagon it couldn't have happened. And fifty years ago the horn would have been a Klaxon, operated by squeezing the rubber bulb. The trouble is that life keeps getting complicated to the point where the average person can't cope with it."

There were dubious depths in her eyes. "I wouldn't say we've quite reached that point," she said. "The button's right there on the dash, and I should think anybody of average intelligence could cope with it . . . If you don't mind trying."

"Oh. Yuh, sure."

I ranged up for a look-see into this nest of leather, chromium, and plastic. The seat upholstery was of cream leather, and on the cushion lay a transparent gadget bag that contained a swimmer's glass-faced mask and a snorkel tube—the kind with a ping-pong-ball valve at the upper bend.

"It's next to the post," the girl called.

My glance ran down the steering post and found a plastic-faced envelope enclosing a State of California vehicle registration slip; the law requires such a slip in plain sight, I guess to simplify things for the private dicks. This one said "Avalon Gage" and "555 Ynez Terrace."

I pushed the button, and the convertible's hood made with an alligator yawn.

"Better let me put it down this time, Miss Gage," I called. Of course it might have been Mrs. Gage, and I sort of waited to be corrected there.

But apparently she hadn't noticed. "I guess you think I'm an awful dope, getting hung up like that." She was peering down and brushing her hands over a grime stain that only a good dry cleaner had a chance of removing.

"No, I don't. I think you're one woman in a million to even know how to begin to disconnect a horn, Miss Gage." There was no wedding ring on her hand, at least.

"I was engaged to a hot-rodder once," she said. "Put in an entire summer hanging around a garage and passing him valve-lifters and things."

No engagement ring, either.

I hadn't gotten around to doing anything about the hood. She reached past me and banged it down. "Thanks so much . . ."

She tossed that briskly—or was it brusquely?—and slid past, inserting herself under the convertible's wheel. She looked different there—relaxed, smiling a competent smile. Brisk or brusque, it spelled brush-off.

One of the prettiest girls I'd ever met, too, even if filthy rich. Probably nothing to do but loll on the beach and sport around in her five-to-six-thousand dollars' worth of dreamboat.

"Been a pleasure. I enjoyed it, Miss Gage."

"Mrs. Gage," watching to see how I took the news.

I pulled a long face—not for any personal reason, fundamentally; it was just that it's a matter of professional advancement that I train myself to make accurate observations and correct inferences.

"Ava runs the Gage Travel Agency. I work for her. And I've

got to refund some unused air transportation, get back before the banks close, too. So long, thanks again."

The convertible pulled past me, without breaking any glassware. I watched it take the curve ahead like the easy-gliding swoop of a tropical, exotically plumaged bird.

She worked for a living. Pounded keyboards, answered phones, ran errands. Well, I had known those TV hoity-toities were to be taken like the commercials.

Then I noticed the screwdriver on the pavement. The girl had dropped it, most likely while trying to brush the grime from her skirt, and afterward had been in too much of a rush to remember. So I plodded to the wagon and opened the glove compartment and drew out the canvas-bound notebook. "Gage Travel Agency," I jotted.

There was something else to make a note of, and after frowning a second I recalled what—*scopophiliac*. I meant to look it up the first crack I got at a dictionary.

Just as I had feared, the hand brake stuck, and I had to uncoat and up-sleeves to work on it. The girl came tearing back down the hill about the time I finished. As she came near I stuck out my arm and waved the screwdriver at her.

She must not have noticed; she probably took the gesture as a friendly parting wave.

TWO

UP THERE on the hilltop lay a large-acreage estate surrounded by an aging brick wall, six feet high to the planter top, in which bristled a yard-tall growth of cactus. Looking for local color, I admired the texture of the grout-stained brick and the weirdly stark patterns of the spike-thrusting cactus. But if I had been a burglar or a kidnapper casing the layout, I would have seen this wall to be a barrier just as tough as industrial mesh fence surmounted by barbed wire.

Lime trees grew inside, upper branches dripping bar fruit; globular oranges hung on larger trees; ornamentals offered flowers the size of teacups. And in the middle, a roof as big as that of a Minnesota dairy barn, only covered with thick shake shingles. I came to a driveway barred by twin cast-iron gates. More curlicued iron overhead formed the initials HHC.

I nosed the wagon in, stepped down, and fumbled at the gates. They were locked. I peered through the bars, along a curving avenue of roses—big hothouse explosions of yellow, salmon, and lipstick shades.

"Hi, Buddy," I called.

Buddy was no kid, he was sixty-plus, a stocky figure in khaki
pants and a leather-sleeved jacket, bald, and with the kind of thick,
resolute face that belongs on old family servitors. He broke off his
worshipful kneeling at the base of a Revlon-hued specimen.

"This the Crossway castle?" I halloed.

He headed my way, swinging hands gloved in lineman's gaunt-
lets. The right carried a pruning clipper that went *ka-snip, ka-snip.*
He had the appearance of a combination chauffeur, handy man,
and possibly superannuated bodyguard. This last I gathered from
his eyes, which were those of a bouncer about to ask me to leave
quietly or be thrown out.

"What are you selling?" he called in a voice that didn't want any.

"It's all right . . . The name's Svederup. Ken Svederup. The lord
of the manor expects me."

He stopped, six or eight yards short of the gates. His toe kicked
at the driveway. "See these metal strips? It's the same on your side.
Drive over them and the lock works automatically.

It worked just as he said, the gates swinging apart and reclosing
as the wagon's tires crunched over the inner strips.

"Thanks, Pop," I said through the window.

"Park by the pool." His voice thinned behind me.

I drove on. The rose-bordered driveway swung right, swung
left, and threw a loop around a swim pool separated from the
house by a golf-green lawn. Sprinklers were playing, and a rain-
bow danced. Very pretty, but how was I to reach the house?

The latter impressed me as being about a twenty-room replica
of a European chateau, architectured in the exposed-beam and
stucco style. The former were painted blue, the stucco tinted
lemon, and the trained and intervaled vines flung out sprays of
scarlet.

I sized it up through the Leica view-finder, including the king-
sized centerpiece of a pool done in blue- and lemon-colored tiles.
But it needed a movie shot, to get the wind skittering sprinkler
drops across the pool's surface.

Buddy, or Pop, came along—I expected to valve off the artificial
rain storm.

"You didn't fly," he remarked.

Some of those old servitors consider themselves practically members of the family. Ungloved now, this one twiddled a cabbagehead
of yellow rose as he eyed the Chevie wagon.

"You drove in *that* all the way from Milquevais?" He gave the
place name a French pronunciation. Back home, we say "Milky
Way," and speak of our burg as the Cottage Cheese Capital of the
World.

But how in heck would H. H. Crossway's hired help know I

hailed from Milquevais? A bubble of suspicion ballooned in my mind. I peered closely at Buddy, or Pop, or was he . . . ?

What I had to go on was the framed photograph hanging in the Milquevais *Globe* editorial office, an iron-maned, granite-jawed, captain-of-industry face over a silver plate inscribed: "Founder and President, Crossway Press, Inc."

The old codger looked enough like it to be a member of the family—a distant, indigent relative living here on the President and Founder's largess.

"Yuh, I drove out," I said. "My vacation was due, and I took off a week early and looked in on Yellowstone and Zion National Parks."

He regarded me with rather grim, faded, blue denim eyes.

"It's been a hell of a week," he said.

That office wall photograph could have been taken ten to fifteen years ago. Possibly an airbrush had firmed the jowls and placed a high-powered executive gleam in the eyes.

Anyway, Buddy or Pop resembled that photo as much as the average politician looks like his campaign poster portrait.

He must have observed suspicion in my manner. "I mean, you must have found those places terribly crowded—reservations sold out months in advance," he explained.

I put him to the test. "There's always room for one more, as the cow said when she put her foot in the milk pail."

If he had smiled at the crack, I would still have put him down as an unemployed relative. But his face was dead-pan.

"A guy can always squeeze in if he's willing to bunk in the car, light the propane, and dump a package of dehydrated soup in the pot." I stepped behind the wagon, lowered the tailgate, and showed him the groceries and Kamp Kit stashed in under the plywood frame of the air mattress bed.

All the time, I studied him, and he studied me. "You're a rugged outdoorsman, evidently," he commented.

"We all have our hobbies. And I guess yours must be roses."

He nodded with vigor.

"Raise 'em with your own hands, I see."

Another nod. "Yes, the gardeners aren't careful. They carry spores of various fungus diseases on their clothes. These roses are my own varieties. You might be interested in the latest . . ." He held up the yellow specimen as a young mother offers her infant, to be seen and cooed over but not touched. "I'm thinking of naming it the Billy Graham. . . ."

I knew now, from the way his jaw jutted and his eyes charged with blue sparks of personal-magnetism electricity.

Should I apologize for my mistake?

Maybe he was a little deaf and hadn't heard clearly. He must have been past the mid-century mark when that photo was taken, and probably now could have qualified for Social Security if he'd needed it. His hand with the glove stripped off showed arthritic gnarling.

"Suppose we sit down," he said.

With senior-citizen caution, he lowered into the nearest poolside chair. I hiked up the imported Italian pure silk knees to save the crease and settled into the next nearest.

He stared at the pool, seemed to be prompted by it. "I'm given to understand, Svederup, you're a swimming champion."

Well, once I did win the Lake Milquevais Annual Cheese Day Swim. But how come he'd ever heard of that?

"Dive a bit, by any chance?" he pursued.

"I can jump in headfirst. Nothing graceful or acrobatic."

"I mean skin diving. 'Goggle fishing,' I believe it's sometimes called. Underwater spearing and hunting. Any experience along that line?"

"No, sir. Ours is a mud-bottom lake, and down on the floor you'd only kick up a lot of silt. Besides, in warm weather the water turns green with algae."

"Still, you're young enough to learn."

I said nothing. If I had spoken my thoughts, there were other abilities I would rather have mastered. The truth is, I've always wanted to be a writer.

Only, I've also liked to eat. That was why, a couple of years ago, I'd gone to work as a reporter on the Milquevais *Globe*. I never mentioned my aspirations there, however, because it's the sort of thing you play hush-mouth until you've produced a best seller. Or at least until you've sold something somewhere.

H. H. C.'s voice gruffed a bit. "It seems you have certain talents as an investigator."

I knew where he got *that* idea. Back home, we'd this sort of crazy taxi-driver and bootlegger, Canadian Jones, who shotgunned to death a Minneapolis flour-mill salesman. And when the manhunt was several days old, the thought came to me Canadian might be lying low on one of the little cattail islands up at the sloughy end of the lake. None of the islands was any bigger than a tennis court, but a man could hide in the reeds and brush willow and live on roots and bulbs and frogs. With the advantage that before being seen, he could blow the head off anyone who came poking around in a boat. I took the notion of swimming out there after dark and before moonrise.

"Frankly, Mr. Crossway, that was all luck"—just my good fortune that the moon, when it came up, was behind Canadian instead of silhouetting me.

"Luck?" You'd have thought from his voice it was a dirty word. Nobody with a million bucks in the bank believes luck plays much part in life, I guess.

"No," said the old boy, "it took more than mere luck to extract a confession from that scoundrel. Obviously you're pretty good at getting people to talk, open up with their inmost confidences and motives. . . ."

But what else had there been to do but talk after I'd managed to tie up Canadian with his bootlaces? The mosquitoes wouldn't let us sleep, and we'd the whole night to spend before I could find the killer's boat he had sunk in five feet of water. All I did was probe him for the motivations any writer would need to know in connection with a character committing a murder.

That's the low-down on how the Milquevais *Globe* and the thirty-seven other Crossway Press newspapers came to scoop the Twin Cities and Chicago dailies with the capture and confession.

Later I got a letter of congratulation signed by H. H. Crossway, with a bonus check and the news I'd won the Monthly Expense-Paid West Coast Trip Award.

The award generally went to a circulation manager or advertising salesman. The lucky winner went to La Jolla to receive a citation from H. H. C. personally, went to Hollywood for lunch with some starlet who wanted the country newspaper publicity, went to some TV shows, finished at San Francisco full of Fisherman's Wharf food and ambition to again break all circulation or advertising sales records.

Well, it was free. And worth it, if a guy could work in Yellowstone and Zion and maybe the Grand Canyon on the return trip.

Then a crack like a kid's Fourth-of-July pistol startled me, but it was only Mr. Crossway hooking one knee over the other. He must have stiffened up at his rose gardening.

"You have the same strange effect on me, Svederup, and old as I am, I feel tempted to take down my hair—in a manner of speaking—and give vent to my—er—personal problems."

I wondered what this was all about. Maybe I should have felt flattered, but I turned as uncomfortable as the bridegroom in a command-performance wedding.

"I'm a rich man, yes," he soliloquized. "But a happy man, no. I'm lonely; I've found nothing except bitter disappointment at life's end."

I guess what got under my hide was the Big Brass attitude. His idea that naturally I'd share his sorrows over the things his money wouldn't buy. Well, what if I had opened up on *him*—remarked that he looked like an understanding, fatherly old man, and I wanted him to bend an ear to *my* personal problems? He'd have blown the whistle fast, you bet. Sympathy between a rich old publisher and a poor young reporter is a one-way street, and I wanted to detour it.

"Mr. Crossway," I said, "you don't even know me."

"I think I know you pretty well, Svederup. You remind me so much of my own son. . . ."

I reminded him of Junior? I figured he must be crazy, figured the locked gates and cactus-topped wall were to keep him from running at large. I even peeked around to see if there wasn't a good husky attendant lurking in the shrubbery.

It must have been I had subconsciously overheard a rustle or a caught breath. Because there *was* a face peeping around from behind the Chevie wagon—the most utterly beauteous, sensuous, alluring face I ever gazed on, before or since. The features I can't describe except in clichés: a perfect oval face with aristocratically high cheekbones, eyes that were wells of Oriental mystery, lips shaped in a Cupid's bow carved in pink-flesh fruit.

There are dames that a man has to go *for* or go *against*. I jumped up. I wasn't tearing out my hair at sight of her, just trying to doff the hat I happened not to be wearing.

THREE

SHE'D BEEN SEEN, so she came out from behind the wagon.

A beach cape floated off her shoulders, with nothing but a string at the throat to keep it from blowing completely away.

Underneath, she was clad in a Bikini, consisting of a loading-platform bra—it held up without covering up—and a breechcloth which narrowly escaped being a mere G-string.

Well, this was a private pool. I imagine she could legally have gone into it naked if she'd wanted to.

I could see the old man wasn't too overjoyed by the new developments. "Mr. Svederup," he mumbled. "My daughter-in-law, Mrs. Crossway."

She was Junior's wife. Or I should say, widow.

"I'm not interrupting anything, am I?" she said.

"Why, no, Nelda," said H. H. C. "Svederup here is the one who pulled off that Minnesota murder scoop. I named him for the Monthly Award tour, and he has arrived to receive his citation."

"Where has he been hiding all week?" said Nelda.

"F' ling?" I said.

"The travel agency which handles the Award tours couldn't locate you," Mr. Crossway said.

That tied in the girl in the convertible.

"Consequently I wasn't expecting visitors," Nelda said. "I only came out for a dip, and the sprinklers being on, I slipped around from the side of the house."

I still thought she had been eavesdropping on us, and I wondered how she reacted to the suggestion that I resembled her husband. I'd seen Junior, once; 'way back in '48, he flew out from Chicago to make the Milquevais Cheese Day speech.

Chicago, I should explain, is headquarters for the thirty-eight Crossway papers, scattered from Illinois through Minnesota in the county-seat towns and smaller cities. The local news and ads are handled in the towns; the solid Republican editorials and patent medicine ads come from Chicago.

By '48, H. H. C. had already more or less retired to California, leaving the active management to Junior.

Junior was a chip off the old block, only more polished. He wore shell-rimmed glasses that gave him a thoughtful, studious air, further softened by a kindly grin. He stood 5-6 in elevator shoes, weighed 180 to 190, had blue eyes and blond hair.

He could write a good speech, and people even read the editorials after Junior started writing them.

That same year—'48—he ran for the Illinois legislature, and toward the end of the campaign, married Nelda, who was Miss Stenographer of '48. She couldn't have cost him any working-girl votes.

I'm quoting the Democrats on Junior, and the above is the worst they could say against him. They feared him as future gubernatorial or even vice-presidential timber, especially if he and Nelda should time a blessed event to occur just before election day. As it turned out, though, Korea happened. Junior got himself accredited as a war correspondent and flew the Pacific to interview MacArthur and get an eye-witness view of the fighting.

His jeep was pinned down by infiltrating Reds. He died bravely: wouldn't let himself be loaded into the rescuing 'copter until the jeep driver had been loaded aboard.

Now, I ask, wherein lay my resemblance to Junior? Physically, I'm a string bean with *brown* eyes and *brown* hair. And our personalities were as different as possible.

For instance, I couldn't be elected dog-catcher, not unless they let the dogs vote. Not even then, since my following would include mostly the stray mutts, disenfranchised by the legal residence requirement.

"Well, Mr. Svederup," Nelda was saying, "how do you like our village?"

Here I was already thinking of her by her first name, also trying to think up some bright answer to impress her.

"Fine, what I've seen so far . . ." That didn't sound half bright even to me. "Only I don't know why a place of 15,000 calls itself a village. Milquevais has 12,302, and we consider ourselves quite the thriving metropolis."

Her eyes showed more than polite interest in our banter. "La Jolla doesn't *want* to be a city," she said. "It has a hamlet complex, wants to remain what it was in the old steam-trolley days."

I got the impression the town was too slow to match her speed. "You mean there isn't much night life, no café society frolics?"

There was a far-awayness in Nelda's beautiful eyes. "I mean I don't believe in living on your yesterdays when there are tomorrows to be conquered." It made me wonder if she had written Junior's speeches and editorials for him.

Anyway, I sensed high-powered urges in Nelda. Ambitious ones. Untamed drives. In fact, I could easily visualize her as a dangerous woman.

The question was what did she see in me?

"Speaking of tomorrows," she went on, "are you just driving through, or planning to stay a few days?"

I noticed H. H. Crossway's gnarled fingers tearing Billy Graham to billy-hell. He must have been really annoyed; I assumed he didn't want me and Nelda getting too well acquainted. He threw away a fistful of yellow petals and heaved himself up from his chair.

"Come inside," he said. "I want to show you the view from the study."

The water curtain was gone.

"How'd you turn that off?" I asked.

"Time meter on the line," he said. "Come along."

The tail of my eye caught Nelda flipping into the pool. She surfaced, lay motionless a moment, then flutter-kicked to the opposite side. In the water she was as sinuous as a water snake.

The study had a picture window with a stubby telescope mounted on a sill tripod, and H. H. C. really insisted on showing me the view. I guess he felt it was a social obligation—same as in Milquevais, where you've got to drive visitors out past the World's Biggest Cottage Cheese Plant. "The Bishop's School," he pointed out. "The Clinic—that's why I came out here originally—the Cove, the Surf and Racquet Club."

I'd already admired La Jolla from the road, so I kept sneaking peeks around the study. It was about the size of the reading room in the public library back home but had classier furniture and souvenirs of Junior hanging around the walls—pictures of him, his college of journalism diploma, his World War II Navy commission, his credentials to the 1948 GOP National Convention.

"The Scripps Institute of Oceanography," Crossway said, winding up the finger-guided tour, "Robert's hangout." He took a deep breath. "Now, getting back to Robert . . ."

Getting *back* to him? "Who's Robert?" I said.

"Why, my son. My younger and only surviving child."

So that was the score. My error. All I knew about the family was what I'd read in the Crossway Press, and there'd never been any mention of a younger son. Maybe this Robert had a criminal record, or was born with two heads—except he was supposed to resemble me!

"Mr. Crossway," I said, "I'm now confused. *What* about Robert?"

The old man's captain-of-industry expression tired into a frustrated, overage master sergeant's look.

"I wish to God I *knew* what about him," said the tycoon. "I've never understood the boy. He's beyond me."

"Oh."

"His mother died an early death. His Aunt Debby, I am afraid, secretly encouraged certain—odd—tendencies in Robert. She herself took long beach walks."

"Hmm," I said.

"Robert started by collecting seashells as a boy, and now, as a grown man, he counts the plankton in jellyfish stomachs."

"Plankton?"

"Plants and animals in the ocean," he said, "and Robert is doing oceanographic research at the Institute here. As a graduate student. They don't pay him; he pays for the privilege. . . ."

"Is that bad?"

The old denim eyes gave me a long, drab, sobering stare.

"I won't live forever, Svederup," he said. "And in fairness to my employees and nearly half a million subscribers, I cannot safely bequeath the Crossway Press to a total stranger who happens to bear my name but who in his business inexperience might bankrupt the enterprise in a year."

He paced to his study desk. It was mahogany, and almost as long as a bar. He broke open a humidor of cigars.

I always accept a free cigar: the next man I meet might like one. But this torpedo made such a bulge in the imported Italian pure silk coatfront that I slipped it back into the humidor. Mr. Crossway, bending over the flame of a solid gold, soup-tureen-sized lighter, failed to notice.

"Things came to such a pass some seven years ago that I was obliged to cut off and disinherit Robert. . . ."

I lifted an eyebrow.

"Well, I was a younger man then, and Robert was a younger man. I frankly hoped the experience would have a chastening effect and he would settle down and consent to a reconciliation. But he never enters under this roof except for the once-a-year family dinner in commemoration of his mother's birthday, and those occasions always end in a quarrel."

I said nothing. I don't wear my collar backwards, and the air mattress in my wagon is not a psychoanalyst's couch.

The President and Founder blinked at me through a fog of cigar smoke. "It isn't just the money, Svederup. Even if I were a poor man, I'd like to be closer to my own flesh and blood before I pass on . . ."

He coughed, and not merely because the Havana was too rich for his constitution. He had a father's heart bleeding on his sleeve; I could tell, as he acted so damned furtive and ashamed of the emotion.

Of course he could also have had something hidden up that sleeve, and it occurred to me . . .

"I repeat that I don't know Robert, and if I knew more about him, I would understand better how to make one more effort. . . ." He sighed, shook off the sentimentality, and became practical. "Svederup, what's your present salary on the *Globe*?"

"Seventy a week." One reason for the Award is that the Crossway papers do not notoriously overstimulate the employees pecuniarily.

The cigar made a gesture of knighting me. "I'm taking you off the payroll as of now," said H. H. C. "You'll stay here in La Jolla, at a hundred a week and expenses. Your assignment will be to get next to Robert, penetrate his shell, find out *all* about him, draw him out as you did Canadian Jones. And report to me."

Well, it struck me as a bit high-handed. Like Ol' Massa yanking a field hand out of the cotton patch and making him over into a house flunky.

"I'll buy the first half," I said.

He looked puzzled.

"You can fire me off the payroll, boss," I said, "but you can't turn me into your stool pigeon."

Mr. Crossway gave the impression of going to bite the cigar in two, swallow half and spit the rest into my face. But blamed if he didn't break into a grin, and what was harder, twinkle out of those well-washed denim eyes.

"I was right about you," said the old man. "That's just the way Robert would react. Be insulted, fly off the handle, *be* insulting. . . . You two are *exactly* alike. Both unmarried, the same age, the same interest in water sports, the same pride. You will be buddies with him in no time."

"Only I don't want the job."

It wasn't so much the pride; telling him off satisfied that part. Back in Milquevais I'd learned to remain a respectful distance from other people's family feuds, and especially where these feuds revolve around wills and inheritances. You might as well stick your neck into a buzz saw. And now I had a sixth-sense feeling of danger, and a common-sense feeling that this time the moon wouldn't rise when and where I needed it.

"You wouldn't be spying on my son," said the old man. "You'd be doing him the greatest possible favor."

"How?"

"Look at it this way, Svederup. You're a long way from home
and family; you probably know the sensation of homesickness.
Now, suppose you were estranged from all your family perma-
nently and had no home to return to and along came a clean-cut
new friend to patch up the old wounds, reunite the family
ties . . ."

He was a shrewd psychologist—as he'd had to be to turn a little
country print shop into a newspaper empire.

Or was he so shrewd?

"It won't work," I said. "Robert won't unbosom himself to a
Crossway reporter."

"Nobody need know who you are, where you came from . . ."

"They already know," I said.

"Nelda?" he asked. "Don't worry, she's loyal."

Loyal to whom? to what? I thought. But I said, "The travel
agency."

"The travel agency doesn't even know your name," he said.
"The agency air-mailed a plane ticket to the *Globe* managing editor. He sent it back. That's all. Anyway, the Award winners always leave the next day for Hollywood. It's routine, happens
every month, causes no curiosity whatsoever."

He had it all planned, how he'd bring me out here and size me
up, and if I looked the right size, slip me the shrewd psychological
sales talk.

"Robert's lonely, too. As you'd be. He'll feel about this as you'd
feel if someone were to cure a family quarrel and perhaps make
you the heir to five million dollars. . . ."

Well, as I say, I knew about this kind of family quarrel, and in
this case the stakes were bigger and the buzz saws would be bigger
and sharper and more of them around. And run by electric eyes or
radar so as to saw the man in two automatically.

"Put yourself in his place; think of yourself as Robert . . ."

I even recognized the psychological appeal: identification. The
bait on the hook was Robert—*who was supposed to be so much
like me!*

"Mr. Crossway, I won't promise a word. But I guess while I'm
here, I might at least look into the thing." I couldn't help looking
into it any more than you can help glancing into a full-length mirror.

FOUR

THE TROUBLE with hunches is they don't last. Here I had this
premonition of buzz saws and booby traps, and yet by the time I
parked on Ynez Terrace, it might all have been something I ate

the night before. And a hunch like that hadn't much chance on Ynez Terrace.

The terrace had been a curve of residential street in the steam-trolley era Nelda mentioned. They had left the glossy privet and scarlet blooming tropicals, and had turned it into a street of medical and legal and tax service offices without resorting to any flashy modern architecture.

Number 555 was typical. It had a front of softly silver-stained vertical cypress flanked by recessed doorways with two narrow, horizontal, tilt-glass display windows. The one door belonged to "Briggs, Burton & Leppner, Members N.Y. Stock Exchange," and that window contained a subdued bulletin board announcing that Dow Jones industrials had gone up 7.42.

The Gage Travel Agency window offered tasteful invitations to visit Acapulco, Norway, and the Balearic Islands. Inside the agency door ran a counter, with a redheaded woman behind it, facing a bearded character in a bullfighter blouse, Bermuda shorts, and Japanese clogs.

"I don't know, Ava, if I can afford Madagascar this year. The way the Big Board is acting up, I don't feel I should risk getting so far out of touch."

He had it tough: if the market had been going down, he couldn't have afforded it, either.

"There's always Paris," the woman said, in such a musical voice that I took a good look her way.

You don't often run across a redhead with such a face that you forget the hair color. It was true of Ava Gage, though. Say you had a favorite grandmother, and one day you found a picture taken when she was a young, charming woman. You wouldn't say, "Some looker, hot stuff." She must have been a wonderful person, you'd think, and that's how I reacted to Ava.

"I suffered through six weeks of Paris last year." The Beard was clamoring for more sympathy.

Ava seemed to enjoy running a Travelers' Aid for the bored. "You should try some side trips to the little off-the-beaten-path places," and she started pencil-sketching these side trips on a map with such enthusiasm that I took alarm. How hard would she have worked at delivering the plane ticket to a Crossway Award winner?

I proceeded downcounter, to where the brunette—brownette —assistant sat stroking a typewriter. She'd changed costumes and looked cool and crisp in a candy-stripe blouse and linen skirt.

"Lost and found department?" I asked.

"I beg your pardon?" said she.

"Here's your screwdriver."

"Oh, thanks. You can just put it down any place . . ."

"Also I'm looking for the information desk."

Actually, I was cooking up a strategy for meeting Robert Cross-way in a natural, off-hand way, instead of tackling him in the Fuller Brush, foot-in-the-door style.

The girl came to the counter. "If I can help, I suppose I owe you the favor."

"I'm a writer," I said, "and I need some local color material."

She didn't look too impressed; I imagined she was too used to celebrated authors stalking the streets.

"We don't have anything here but Chamber of Commerce hand-outs," she said, "and, anyway, hasn't La Jolla already been written up rather extensively? The local color has been pretty well pan-washed by previous prospectors, podner."

"Look," I said, "do you happen to know Mr. Jonathan Latimer?" naming one of the literary celebrities alluded to in the *Geographic*, or *Holiday*, or both.

"Oh, Jack Latimer," she said. "I know of him."

"And Ray Chandler?"

"I never heard him called anything but Raymond Chandler."

"Dr. Seuss?"

"*His* real name's Ted Geisel."

"Max Miller, then." She didn't give me any correction there, so I went on: "No, you don't know them personally, and it follows they don't know *you* personally, and you're virgin territory."

That didn't sound quite the way I meant it, so I added:

"Speaking in the strictly literary sense."

Which wasn't too much of an improvement.

"What I'm trying to say is, I'm thinking of doing a piece on the local water sports, skin diving and so on."

"You must find writing hard work if that's the way you express your thoughts," the girl said. "There's a sport shop two blocks over; you could ask there."

"I'm more interested in the human experience, noncommercial angle," I told her, "and I noticed some of your gear in the car."

"Not my field. That's Brad's stuff . . . Wait a minute!" doing a double-take. "Brad might be human interest for you. Come on back and see."

I stepped through a swinging counter gate, then down a hall-way, and followed the girl guide through a rear door into a back-yard equipped with swings and a teeter-totter and a slide that had a kid up at its top, reading a comic book.

"Oh, Bradley," she said.

The kid came down the slide, reading his book all the way, or looking at the pictures—he hardly struck me as old enough to do much reading. Six or seven. Red hair like Ava's, blue eyes, freckles, a hole where a front tooth belonged.

"Man here wants some dope on skin diving," the girl said to him. And to me: "Say, what is your name?"

"Svederup," I said. "What's yours?"

Before she could reply, the laddie piped in: "Scuba?"

I thought he was trying to say, " 'Scuse me?" the way they do in the primary-grade group, lisping through lacking front teeth.

"Kenneth Svederup," I pronounced carefully.

"Scuba," he repronounced just as carefully. "Self-Contained Underwater Breathing Apparatus. Also activities involving same. That what you want to ask me about?"

The brownette slipped away, leaving me alone with the Brain.

"We'd better start with a discussion of the apparatus," he teed off. "First, the mask. I'd recommend a plate-glass one in preference to plastic, and if you're going to be serious, make it pure gum and shatterproof."

"Huh?"

"And a snorkel."

"Uh huh."

"Fins. Let me suggest you'd be happier with the rigid type of heel-enclosing fin."

"Sure, I wouldn't want to be guilty of dragging around in limp fins."

"Are you kidding me?" he said severely.

I denied it.

"Well, if you're interested, you'll sooner or later want a suit. A wet one will do; the oceanic temperatures here really don't require dry dress."

"What's the difference?"

"The dry excludes water, silly; the wet lets it in."

"Where's the advantage to that?" I said.

"Only a little is admitted and confined, so that your body warms it," Brad explained. "That brings up the next item—lungs that supply compressed air to the diver. And, oh—I almost forgot—either a spear or, better still, an arbalete."

"Come again?"

"The arbalete is a type of crossbow gun designed for underwater shooting," Brad said. "And I honestly think you'd better take some lessons before venturing into the depths with all this stuff you don't even know the names of."

Of course I had been deviously leading his six- to seven-year-old intellect to make that very suggestion.

"Who are some of the outstanding local experts that might slip me a few tips?"

He answered like any kid. "I guess my dad knows more about it than anybody else in the whole world."

His dad would do fine. Anybody would do who belonged to the aquatic set and would pass the word around I was a visiting writer seeking undersea stuff. Eventually, then, I could encounter Robert Crossway without being asked for my credentials.

But if I could get this kid's parents to accept me, I'd be over two hurdles at once, for it would prove Ava didn't suspect my real identity, too.

"Only my dad's awfully busy and can hardly spare the time to teach me even," Brad said.

"Yuh. Well, now, what'd the young lady say was her name?"

"She didn't, but it's Kelly—Clara Kelly. Everybody calls her plain Kelly."

"Then," I said, "let's ask plain Kelly if you can come along to the sports shop and help me buy all these items."

"We'll have to ask Mummy," he said.

I would have sold a lot of mothers the idea of Brad being featured in a famous national magazine. But face to face with Ava—Brad's mother—you couldn't pull anything that phony.

She was older than Kelly—might have been nearer forty than thirty. But what counted was the tranquil candor in her eyes that, if I'd tried anything devious, would have made me feel like the original Yellow Kid.

And she was smart enough to see I was no habitual borrower of young boys. "Mmm," she said, "don't buy him any bubble gum —bad for his teeth. And we close here around five."

I drove Brad to the sports shop, and we loaded up the station wagon with the unbreakable plate-glass face mask and tube and foot-fins and foam Neoprene waterwear, and also some refinements such as a depth gauge and weight-slugged belt Brad and the dealer agreed could come in handy. Signing over the traveler's checks, I was glad all this went onto an expense account.

The marketing binge took time, especially as I stalled along hoping to catch Kelly knocking off her day's work. Florrie Schultz beats the *Globe*'s old files for background dope; she knows all the facts the newspaper never printed in past years. And I thought Kelly might know more about La Jolla than just the literary colony's right names.

But when I dropped Brad at the agency, his mother was sitting out in front in the pink and cream convertible.

"Hurry, darling. Daddy's at the beach, and he expected you at five."

It was five-ten then.

I had missed Kelly, so I tagged Ava from Ynez Terrace to Torrey Pines Road and north up the coast line. She was a good driver, made all the arm signals. Left onto the shore road, and on to where the Don Diego character gestured: "Institute of Oceanography." I was right behind Ava pulling into the grounds.

They had some lovely landscaped effects here, surrounding some buildings as old as the Milquevais opera house, and others as new and stylish as the Milquevais Consolidated High School.

The convertible slid behind ornamental shrubs, and Brad

jumped out and skedaddled for a shanty-like structure on the bluff looking out over the ocean.

I walked up to Ava. "Mrs. Gage," I said, "I feel responsible for Brad's tardiness, and I wish to apologize to you and your husband."

She was extremely nice. "Why, gracious!" she said. "It's not your fault. I knew where to find Brad, but the truth is I became lost in a problem of my own."

"Oh," I said.

"Some poor guy in the Middle West seems to be losing his chance at a wonderful all-expense tour," Ava said.

"Isn't that *his* problem?" I asked.

"It worries me," she said. It worried me, too. But then Brad came up, dragging his feet and with a nervous tremble to his underlip. "Daddy didn't wait. He's gone."

"Don't cry," Ava said, "Daddy hasn't ever disappointed us yet, has he? He may be down on the rocks. We'll see."

She started off, holding onto one of Brad's hands. I seized the chance of helpfully bringing along the junior model fins and mask and snorkel.

We footed it along a driveway, between the parking lots surrounding the ultra-new aquarium.

"This must be an interesting place for your husband to work," I said.

"Steve doesn't work here," Ava Gage said. "I sometimes wish he did. I imagine the Institute staff are really much happier than the real estate and property management people in the village."

On our left, the pier thrust out into the breakers. It marched out on big creosoted pilings to a terminus shed housing some kind of a winch setup. A gate and a "Keep Off" sign barred the pier, and we went past it onto a ramp toward the beach below.

Brad ran ahead. Ava, because of her high heels, took my arm.

"La Jolla is so full of retired successful men trying to find something to fill their empty lives. Steve and I mean to see Brad doesn't take that path."

"Nobody on the rocks," Brad said. You could tell that to him his old man was the greatest, but still this experience hurt.

"He may be farther along," Ava said, releasing my arm while the kid raced ahead along the damp, hard-packed sand.

The long blue waves moved in from the sea, feathered themselves into headdresses of white spray, and then flattened out on the shore. Birds flew up and coasted on unmoving wings just above arm's reach from our heads. And a cool, salt-smelling breeze pushed us along toward the wet, shiny rock slabs that progressed seaward from the base of towering cliffs.

"I only wish Steve could have more of this."

Myself, I couldn't imagine a man having to kill himself to sell real estate within hailing distance of such scenery.

"Help," a voice said. "Help!"

My eyes leaped ahead to the kid.

Brad had wheeled. He was peering out beyond the rocks, a hand shielding his eyes. I looked in the same direction.

A round black doughnut was tossing around out there, a hundred and fifty to two hundred yards offshore. A big wave rolled in, and I lost it. The wave burst with a rumble that died away and left momentary silence.

"Help!" It was a scream this time, and I saw a hand flail the air beside the doughnut. Next I looked again at Brad, for he was screaming, too.

"It's dad!" the kid hollered. "That's daddy's voice!"

Well, as I say, I'd had the hunch, not just a gastric hangover resulting from overindulgence. Which made it worse, because now I knew it *was* a hunch, and was coming true, and there was no hope at all of a happy ending.

FIVE

THE WATER seemed to change, to take on a blue-steel sheen. It'd been scenery seconds before, and now it'd become tons of elemental force hammering on the shore's battlement of wet, glistening, sullenly crouching rocks.

Tough babies, these rocks, armored with barnacles, but the thought crossed my mind they were losing their war— being slugged and smashed faceless, ground into sand by the sea. The sea always wins; give it time—that thought crossed my mind, too.

I bent over and broke a shoelace trying to get out of my boots fast.

"It *does* sound like Steve's voice," Ava Gage said in what seemed a queerly unconcerned tone.

She'd clambered up onto the nearest slab to strike a teetering, tiptoe balance, and her face seemed only mildly interested.

"Don't stand there!" I yelled at her. "Run! Call the cops—lifeguards—Coast Guard . . ."

Big-mouthed me! Brad burst into sobs.

Ava jumped off the rock, caught the kid's shoulders, bent her red head down close.

"Daddy's all *right*," she said in a very quiet, very sure voice. "He has an inner tube to hang onto, hasn't he? So there." Then off she dashed at a jerky, spike-heeled sprint.

I slung my own shoes up the beach, where they'd hardly landed before a gull made a three-point landing to investigate. Other birds were twittering overhead, and between the booms of the exploding surf a voice barely louder than the bird cries was pleading, "Help, help . . ."

Brad was sniffling, mopping tears off his freckles. I gave him a comforting whack on the fanny. "You heard your mummy," I said, "and your mummy's a very wise woman."

I'd never thought of the imported Italian pure silk as a warm fabric, but it was amazing how chilly the breeze blew as I bared my legs.

Finally I made the Danish gingham shirt into a ball that I slung after the other articles of clothing. Stripped to shorts and socks, I picked my way out over the boulder tops, wading through tidepool basins that were whiskered with marine growths and leggy sea insects. The tide pool water felt about the same temperature as Lake Milquevais in the early spring.

Then I came to the jumping-off place, a last foot-hold of rock, washed around by a greenish seethe of sea, too foam-flecked to reveal whether there might be more boulders underneath.

The victim had stopped calling, and the doughnut seemed to be riding the swells farther out than I'd estimated—as if there might be an undertow or rip current giving it a wrong-way ride.

The worst of the deal for my money was the surf that came bursting in, one roller on the other's heels—so fast I couldn't see a prayer of finding an interval of quiet water.

I did a little hesitating, a little idle longing for the newly purchased fins stowed away in my wagon. Just as I'd told H. H. C., I'd never done any scratching of Lake Milquevais' bottom; but I *had* tried webbed feet on the surface, and I knew that with them even an average swimmer could beat Olympic-trials records.

Then I jumped in, feet first.

About the third stroke, I came on top of a comber, got swamped by it, got slapped back onto the rock edge, hung on there, with a pint of salt water strangling my throat, a ringing in my ears, blood running out of a forearm scraped on the rock. That wave had really had a ball with me.

And there was no time to rest between rounds—not if I wanted to do any good. It was shove-off, four strokes, and another wall of water falling like a house on me. This one I had the sense to dive under. It passed overhead in a vast sloshing stampede. Daylight gleamed ahead, and I grabbed breath and barreled away four more strokes, then slid under the next breaker. The third was just a giant swell, and I went up it on one side and down the other.

Now all that remained was to dig in and belt—and fight the stomach-pit sensation of being too late and too slow. Actually, mine isn't a racing crawl: the leg action has a tendency to slide out of the flutter-beat into a semitrudgeon style, and the arms' tempo suggests a tramp chopping wood for his supper.

"Help!"

Brother, I'm hurrying, wearing myself out hurrying!

But why don't I begin to catch some second wind? It was like baseball: some days a man can't warm up properly, and his curve won't break right, and they have to send him to the showers. What a swimmer gets in these circumstances is a cramp.

"Help!"

I could hear him plainly now, and he sounded fretful, like the passengers at the R.R. station fuming while the thirty-minutes-overdue 4:17 comes slowpoking around the bend.

He was probably watching me. I could see him, a hand on the inner tube, and a face-plate flashing its reflection on the water beside him.

No. *Two* face-plates! I broke the crawl-beat at the finish to rise up, treading water, and I saw there were two men, one hanging onto the tube with one hand and using the other hand to keep his companion's face above the waves.

I shot a look at the fellow being helped, first, to see how bad off he was. He'd a mask that'd been pushed or pulled down and rode around his neck. The glass was broken—not broken out like a window but smashed into a spiderweb of white-fissured cracks, like the safety glass in a car accident.

A thatch of wet straw-colored hair cowlicked and covered his right eye. The left eye and the remainder of the face I could see, and they looked bad.

I've had to cover some lake-dragging episodes back home, and when the drowned body comes to the surface I always break into goose flesh. The first look here started my skin to building the same bumps.

That's because timid, morose, ailing people don't as a rule go into the water. The drowning victim is usually a physically healthy, mentally cheerful person who up to the last minute was skylarking around, rocking the boat or diving in too-shallow depths and except for one damn' fool or luckless instant, might have gone on enjoying life another fifty years.

Suspended inside this inner tube was a kind of trap-net device, and in the clear water I could make out that it contained some crustacean shapes—specimens these divers must have been gathering when tragedy struck.

"Help—get him up on the tire."

The rescuer still had on his face mask—a hoop that enclosed his eyes and nostrils but left his mouth free to speak.

Both men were clad in thick, rubbery, black wet half-suits, crotch-length shirts leaving their arms and legs bare.

I grabbed hold of the unmoving one and tried to help hoist him up onto the inner-tube platform.

"Fouled up!" The masked chap had freed his hand, and aimed it in a couple of stabbing downward gestures. "See?"

I dipped my face into the water. With my eyes open and staring into the brine, the shadow dropped by the tube could be seen —the motion of a pair of legs pumping a slow water-walk— deeper down, a streaky flicker leading to a vague, dimly visible torpedo-like object circling under us.

I stuck up my head and yakked: "Shark?" Not that the object looked so very sharklike. The naked eye can't see too clearly under water, though, but I'd never heard of any other fish apt to hang around and maybe attack swimmers. And there was also suspicion that my skinned forearm leaking blood might act as shark lure.

"Bass in tow. Have to cut loose."

The guy hauled a dagger-bladed knife from his suit belt, flipped into a headfirst somersault, and in a moment came up to resheathe the knife.

Now he raised the mask to a forehead rest and threw me a shaky grin. We were on opposite sides of the tube, and I tried to steady the victim's body as the waves lifted and dropped it.

"Better start artificial respiration," a third voice said.

I looked around. Six feet away was a junior-sized mask and a hand waving a snorkel at us.

"Brad!" shouted the man from the opposite side of the tire.

He'd been fairly well under control up to this point, considering what he'd been through before his yells brought help—you wear out fast diving to find and ring up a body from the bottom even of Lake Milquevais. He'd dived a lot deeper than that and was on the edge of exhaustion, and this shout of his sounded more like a scream.

"Brad, go back. Go back, do you hear me?" It was the voice of a panicked man, and I could appreciate why. We'd a drowning victim to rush a couple of hundred yards to a surf-pounded beach, and we didn't need any six-year-old overseer in on the operation.

"Use the diaphragm method," said Brad.

He was cool enough; he had only studied lifesaving in a book or seen it demonstrated in a pool.

"Beat it!"

With the advantage of fins and snorkel, the minnow had given me the headstart and nearly equaled my time. Still, he *was* a minnow. "Stick around, kiddy," I said. "Swim in just ahead of us, and don't get too far ahead." I hadn't any ambition for searching the surf to find him afterward.

"That's what I meant," the other man said, under control again.

"He can swim a bit ahead, you tow the tube, and I'll try to give the respiration."

I hooked a wrist around the tire, started out with a side stroke and a scissors kick. It was slow going: Trying to tow a tube with one man sprawled on and another hanging on is like trying to pull the boxcar from a standing start one-handed.

"Maybe if I put on his fins," I said.

"He lost his. Take mine." Only *he* had his hands full, steadying the body on the tube and trying to belly-pump air into it. So I dropped back to detach his flippers and slide my own feet into them.

They were no fit, too big. But they made the difference it makes when you're hiking along the road and somebody comes along and gives you a lift.

Brad, out in front, had the sense to steer a course for the beach below the rocks. Then, just at the surf line, we met a welcoming party of two lifeguards. They grabbed the load and took off, jet-propelled.

Right there I lost any illusions I had had concerning swimming. And I almost lost my shorts in the rollers, too, but finally staggered ashore holding 'em up at the waistline.

The body was stretched on the sand next to a red jeep, the guards were working over it, half a dozen bystanders were looking on, and Brad was trying to look in by sticking a head through the circling legs.

A half-length wetsuit charged past me, caught the kid's arm, snaked him out of there. "Come 'way, son, don't look at it."

Well, I had him tabbed in my mind as Steve Gage, of course.

I walked up, intending to return his fins, carrying them in the hand that wasn't occupied maintaining decency.

He'd spotted his wife in the crowd.

"God damn it, Ava," he said, "what kind of a mother are you? Letting a child be scared for life by such a sight . . ."

She answered without raising her own eyes from the sight: "It's Bob. It's poor Bob Crossway!"

That I wasn't prepared for, and yet in a way I was, too: my mind had an empty, dark, apprehensive place of the right size to receive that news. Kind of a coffin-sized and -shaped place, because I knew the lifeguards were wasting their efforts: Bob Crossway had been dead when I caught up with him.

So I walked up the beach to where numerous wet, nasty little crabs were making a front room rug of my shirt.

SIX

THE LIFEGUARDS did their best. And the first department re-suscitator expert arrived, and he and the machine did their best. Then a doctor came and pronounced Bob Crossway dead.

I had known it from the beginning, and the time passed like standing by an open grave waiting for somebody to throw in the first shovelful. It helped me understand Steve Gage's shouting at Ava to hurry Brad away from the scene.

Steve stuck it out to the bitter end. A thin, sandy-haired man tanned to the color of an Indian, arms folded across the chest of his half-suit of rubber armor. He had a waterproof watch banded onto his wrist. He didn't look at it once. I noticed that. According to my watch, we were there an hour and nineteen minutes.

Finally, though, he came over to me. "You have a car?" he asked. "Mind dropping me at the Club?"

I drove him to the Surf and Racquet Club, half a dozen blocks distant. We entered the grounds by a palm-lined drive that wound through the velvet greenery of a putting course, circling a pretty reed-rimmed pond where a white-capped nursemaid supervised two little girls feeding bread crumbs to the mallards.

I drove slowly; there were humps in the pavement to bridle down the traffic.

"Any place here," Steve Gage said.

I braked to let him out.

"Well," he said then, "thanks for all you did."

"Thanks for nothing, I'm afraid."

"Not your fault. All my damned fault absolutely."

He had it chewing at him inside, all right. We'd lost the guy, and we both felt it. He had been longer at it, and had pretty nearly come apart at the seams in front of his son, and I could understand he'd feel it worse.

"Come on in," he said. "I imagine we can both use a drink." I took him up on it.

The Club consisted of a row of apartment-like buildings strung along the waterfront. We went in through a front office, where a turnstile halted us while Gage signed me in on the guest register. I spelled the name for him. We walked on past athletes making loud racquet strokes on the enclosed tennis courts, and past a plunge pool in a patio full of tables with Filipinos hustling trayloads of drinks to people at the tables, and on into a bar. After some dodging of strapless gowns and dinner jackets, we found chairs in a far corner.

"Double Scotch," said Steve Gage, "on the quick."

I ordered my usual, a bottle of beer.

Along came a black tie escorting an orchid corsage, the nice healthy faces above smiling recognition at Gage and pretending recognition of me.

"How *are* you wonderful guys?" the orchids asked.

"How are things in the deep blue down under?" the tie asked. They hadn't heard.

We didn't tell them.

The drinks were put down. Steve took a jolt of his Scotch, I a sip of beer that tasted thin compared with the home-state brew I'm used to.

"You know, I've been going in week ends with Bob."

So he'd lost a buddy, and what could I say to that?

"Those are restricted waters up around the pier, closed except to the Institute men for research purposes. The thing is, Bob had too much sense to dive alone, and it just happened today I had a canceled appointment, and I called him up. Which I usually don't weekdays, and if I hadn't today . . ." He phrased all this carefully, weaving a concentrating scowl with flaxen brows that looked almost white against his Indian tan. ". . . Bob'd be alive, and it's absolutely my damned fault he isn't."

His eyes were blue inside of lids lowered defensively.

"When your number comes up," I said, "your number comes up."

He threw in another dollop of the double.

"It also happens I called my wife and told her to have the kid at the beach by five."

"I know."

"When you get a little time off, you're under an obligation to spend some of it with your son."

"Sure," I said. "Right."

"Bob and I went out there late, after four, and come five he hadn't got all the specimens he wanted. And my attitude was that I had to keep the date with my kid—oh, cut it short, ten to fifteen minutes, but be there, on the dot."

His attitude gave this talk a twist that made *me* feel I should have ordered something more fortifying than the beer.

Steve Gage leaned toward me, twisting it in harder without knowing it. "A father owes that much to a son. A parent has to respect a promise, and if he doesn't, the kid gets the idea of being fobbed off. Very serious."

"Yuh," I said.

"It got to be five o'clock, and I told Bob I had to paddle in and meet my kid— Great Christ! I know now I should never have deserted him, even though he was a thoroughly proficient and experienced diver—working at only around thirty-five feet, and with a lung."

Listening to Steve Gage knocking himself out, I felt as if the bar had an air-conditioning unit aiming a cold draft on *my* spine.

"Absolutely all my damned fault, because I left a fellow diver out there by his lonesome, figuring I could be back with him in ten, fifteen minutes at the most."

My skin crawled.

"Making a long story short, I didn't find Brad on the beach. And therefore thinking he might be at the building where we keep our diving gear, I hiked on up there. My ten to fifteen minutes stretched out to twenty or more. And during that time, it happened."

Mentally, I was tagging Ava from Ynez Terrace to the Institute, and taking all of a quarter-hour to do it.

My abstraction passed unnoticed, Steve Gage breaking off to flag our Filipino and order seconds of the same. Then he went on. "Know what an arbalete is?" he asked.

"Spear gun."

"Yes, and we carried one lashed onto the tube. And when I swam back out there, I saw right away it was gone. Bob had a line down from the tube, and I followed it, and ran into that big bass. . . . You know how an arbalete works?"

"Shoots a spear . . ."

"Demountable spearhead," Steve Gage said, "with the line on it. I saw this bass had the spearhead in him, and I went below and found Bob."

His eyes now were like murky blue-green tide-pool holes.

"Point is, it takes time to stalk a fish! And no sportsman lets a wounded one escape to suffer, and so after the shot Bob had gone down there amongst the rocks to make his kill. He'd slipped, got tangled in his line, snagged the damned lung harness— I don't know how. You can write your own ticket on that, for when a man is down there alone any lousy little bad break can pull the string. . . ."

"Tough," I said.

"All my damned fault, because if I'd been there I could have hacked him loose and got him up fast enough."

"Nobody's blaming you."

"All my damned fault, because it takes time to stalk and shoot and chase a fish, and if I'd been back at the end of ten to fifteen minutes, I could have brought him up alive."

The Filipino served the seconds.

"My round," I said.

"Give me the chit," Steve said, and took it and the pencil to sign with. "You're in my home, man. I should have asked you up to the apartment, only Brad's a very gifted kid. He's conscientious, introspective, sensitive to a fault. I would hate to have him hear anything said—make him suspect—you know, his coming late had any application to Bob's death."

I would have sold myself out very cheap. Who would have made a bid on me, though?

Steve Gage pushed me a pinched, peering look. "Do you mind if I ask you something, Svederup?"

"Yuh, what?"

"Well, they don't build change pockets into these shorties. Want to take care of the tip?"

I was big about it, spread a buck bill on the Filipino's tray, the big part being that I had no more expense account coverage. Bob Crossway's death ended the assignment, and tomorrow I'd be taking the southern route for a peek into the Grand Canyon. I thought I might jump into it when I reached there.

Steve raised his Scotch refill but didn't taste it; he put the glass down with a decisive click. "I'm glad we had this talk. It's helped me see what I have to do."

He looked different—determined, his mouth trenched straight and hard across his face.

"I can't let Brad feel any remote responsibility about being late. I'm going to say I was out there with Bob when it happened, and Brad will never know the difference . . ."

His eyes challenged me to make an issue of it.

I couldn't see the issue, myself. Would a six- or seven-year-old kid worry about this thing? start to brooding, *If it weren't for me, Bob Crossway might be alive?*

I didn't know. But I did know that I had to go and tell that old man up on the hill how the last of his line died. "I guess you showed me my duty, too," I said.

And off I went, pretty much in a state of flux mentally, to dine and dial the front office pay phone.

"H. H. Crossway residence," a butlerish voice said.

"I'd like to speak to Mr. Crossway," I said.

"There has been a death in the family," the voice said in a kindly, please-omit-flowers tone. "The family are not receiving any calls. You may leave your name . . ."

I gave it.

"Oh, yes, Mr. Svederup. Mr. Crossway left word to tell you that you have a reservation at Chaparral House, 14-a, and remain there. He'll get in touch with you later."

So I asked the Club office girl where I'd find Chaparral House.

"Three blocks over and two down," she said, "but you'll need a passport with visas to get in there. It's a different country," she said.

"What country?" I asked.

"Texas," she said.

Chaparral House was where some Texan oilman sunk the royalties of a few gushers, and 14-a turned out to be one of a row of glass-faced suites built on a flush level with a flagged courtyard that surrounded a pool lighted by Hawaiian torches.

The interior was nice, too. Fixed up like Hollywood's idea of a $50-a-week working chick's apartment, it had all-over Tartan plaid carpeting, divan and armchairs modeled on fat prize-sheep lines, only plushier, with shin-height cocktail tables with polished petrified-wood tops. The ash trays were in the Mexican metate mode; the lights hung suspended from all-which-way extension rods; and the wall pictures had been painted probably by Communists.

I slipped the bellhop two dollars' bribe to smuggle my battered suitcase in the back way.

Then I retired to the lavender-tiled shower and put in a session with spray and steam. The towel was lavender, likewise, and large enough to have saddle-blanketed an elephant.

Afterward, I opened the suitcase and selected a pair of J. C. Penney's $5.98 drip-and-dry dress pants, also a nylon neck reinforced cotton tee shirt, plus white stretch socks and a pair of arch-supported cushion-tread basketball shoes.

I couldn't decide whether to sneak out for a hamburger or just sit there and chew the cud of spiritual anguish: *Suppose I hadn't roped Brad into being my shopping guide. Suppose I hadn't fooled away time figuring to catch Kelly leaving work.*

Ava Gage had been so nicely polite, assuring me she'd been delayed at her work, anyway. But it wasn't altogether true, because I'd found her parked in the car and waiting to go. And if true, what had been holding her up?

That kid newspaper reporter and his all-expense tour! Except for *that* jerk, Ava would have knocked off early and had Brad down there on the beach by five on the dot. And Steve Gage could have been at the scene while Bob was still alive and fighting his big fish. . . .

Admit it, I said to myself, *the others just had tough luck. The fish happened along to get harpooned. Bob Crossway happened to get tangled up. Steve happened to be ashore at the time. But your part you planned that way.*

Oh, sure, I never intended to kill anybody by it. But that's how it happened, and the good old hometown ensemble of grass-roots country store clothes couldn't keep me from feeling like the villain of the piece.

SEVEN

AFTER WARMING my sins on the fire of remorse a while, I began to realize that it would all have been different if old man Crossway hadn't put me on the assignment.

And if I told him the complete truth, it would be to heap at least the ashes of remorse on his head.

This made me feel better enough to ring room service and order steak *Chateaubriand*, with the chef's salad tossed in Roquefort dressing and the French fries, accompanied by a coffee pot.

If the rich eat like that all the time, I frankly don't know where they put it. I was still only whittling around the edges of the steak when there was a tapping outside the sliding glass door. The room-service waiter had drawn the drapes—to prevent passersby being annoyed by my table manners, probably. *H. H. Crossway in touch*, I thought.

Anyway, I had the last name right, for when I opened up, in glided Miss Stenographer of 1948 to sling a mink stole across the nearest article of furniture.

"I hear you were with Robert when it happened," said Nelda.

Possibly out of respect to Bob's memory she'd attired herself in just one rope of pearls and a black dress.

Black is the color of mourning, but on the other hand what is more titivatingly titillating than black lingerie? It seemed to me this dress of Nelda's ended toward the negligee kind of black, but of course I was seeing her through the wide, impressionable eyes of a young yokel from the dairylands. Not that the girls back home come to the Cheese Day Ball in bustles and hoops, but at least you can tell whether one of them is wearing her party dress or her nightie.

"Quite a coincidence, I might add," said Nelda, viewing me through her odalisque eyes of mystery.

"Or subtract, divide, solve by the square root of the lowest common denominator," I said.

"Whatever that means."

"It means nothing. Start with nothing, and whether you add or subtract or multiply by zero, the answer comes out nought."

I went back to the steak; no sense letting that grow cold.

Nelda parked on the divan's shoulder. "Your mathematics are better than your etiquette," she said.

"*Is* better."

"Oh, my God, I didn't come here for lessons in grammar."

"What did you come for?" I said.

"Why, Robert *died* this afternoon. You were there, and I felt some member of the immediate family should obtain the firsthand details, and it would be less painful for me than for Father Crossway at his age and—you know—everything."

"Did he send you?" I said.

"No, it was my idea of the thoughtful and considerate thing to do."

She sat prettily posed, swinging one black-sheen-hosed leg. About a half-ounce of shiny black leather formed the suggestion of a slipper on her foot.

"I'm sorry," I said. "I wasn't there when it happened, coincidentally or otherwise. You'll have to get the details from Steve Gage."

"But you were in on the rescue. You must know whether Bob was conscious when you reached him, and whether he uttered any last words?"

"Oh, sure."

Her leg stopped swinging, froze with the slipper toe pointing at me. I looked higher up, into Nelda's lovely face. She wasn't giving away any emotional reactions there; it might have been because beauty contestants and politicians' wives learn how to stand up to the flashbulbs and inquiring reporters, and learn how to talk into the mike without their voices trembling.

"Go on," she said without a tremble. "What were Robert's last words?"

"I didn't hear any."

"But you just said . . ."

"I meant, oh sure, I knew whether he was conscious. He wasn't. They only drown once, you know."

Her leg had resumed swinging.

"It might have been a heart attack. Mother Crossway and Aunt Debby both died of heart attacks," she said. "So I wondered."

"Why?" I said. "Had you in mind any particular last words you were expecting?"

"No, except that sometimes at the last minute people in the actual contemplation and peril of death make oral wills. That kind of last-breath bequest has been upheld by the courts, and so I wondered."

Well, I mused, *whether she wraps the package in a Bikini or in black chiffon, underneath's the cold steel..*

"Did he have so much to bequeath?" I said.

"An inheritance from his Aunt Debby," Nelda disclosed. "Income property. Apartment building."

"Again, you'll have to ask Steve Gage. He was holding Bob's head out of the water a while before I arrived."

Nelda's leg again ceased swinging, and this time her toe gave a little wriggle. "We won't mention this to Steve. What Robert

said to him alone, or Steve may say he said, doesn't materially matter. In our state, a valid oral will requires two ear witnesses."

I took her word; I couldn't imagine her being trapped off first
base on a technicality. *Her* weakness consisted of leading from too
much strength, it seemed to me.

"Mrs. Crossway, Jr.," I said, "what are you so afraid of?"

"Afraid?"

"Makes you act this way."

"What way?"

"You're putting up this brazen, ruthless siren act," said I, "like
a poker player with aces up and a mitt full of discards."

"You're wrong," said Nelda.

"Trying to win the big pot on bluff, secretly scared to death
somebody may call you . . ."

Nelda picked up and adjusted her mink. "I was never afraid of
anything in my life."

Just then another drumming of knuckles announced somebody
else outside the draped panes. Nelda flinched as if the mink had
come alive and bitten her neck.

"That sounds like a house dick's knock," she exclaimed, and
took two skating strides and a waltz turn through the bathroom
doorway.

She must have thought I was really a yokel. Why, the Commercial House back home stopped breaking down doors twenty-five
years ago. And what would a lobby snoop be doing in this ultra-
smart motel?

"She knows Father Crossway is due, and doesn't want him to
find her here," I thought. Only what made her think I wouldn't
tell, I wondered on my way to the sliding glass wall.

Blessed if Nelda hadn't been right. Or anyway, less wrong.
There stood a uniform, Hawaiian torchlight flickering on hol-
stered gun butt and tunic badge. "Police Department," came a
hard sober voice from the visor shadow. "You're Svederup, the
writer?"

I reeled a backward step from the shock of premature fame.
He took a forward step and doffed his cap.

"I've read your stuff, and it's great," said the cop.

"It's really nothing, officer," I said.

"The name's Patterson, Pat Patterson. And I still say you turn
out some truly terrific stuff."

He produced a pencil and notebook and looked as though he
meant to request my autograph. But then he said, "Just a few que-
ries concerning that unfortunate tragedy today, Mr. Svederup.
Your home address to start with, please."

I told him.

"Milky Way?" he said, wrinkling his forehead. He had a fine, tall Cro-Magnon forehead, underlaid however by a facial expression more of the Neanderthal era.

"You write science fiction, is that the gag?" he said.

"M-i-l-q-u-e-v-a-i-s," I replied. "Minnesota."

He wrote it down in the book. He now resembled any cop writing out a "where is the fire?" ticket.

"Oh," he said. "A big-shot writer from Milky Way, Minnesota. A real literary star."

"Sinclair Lewis came from a smaller place," said I.

"Yeah. Sauk Center, wasn't it?"

"Oh," I said, "an educated cop."

Officer Patterson regarded me a while. "You write that detective story crap?"

I gave up, I confessed. My undercover assignment had ended anyway.

"I cover the courthouse beat back home, officer. And the church socials and farm auctions, for which I help tack the sales-bills on the telephone posts."

His grin wasn't so Neanderthal; it put him at least into the fairly recent New Stone Age.

"That's better," he said, "and for your information it takes two years' college or the equivalent to get on the San Diego cops nowadays."

"I thought you were a La Jolla cop," I said.

"La Jolla is the substation I work out of, and let me add I broke in by way of the lifeguard service. That much for the qualifying round, now let's get down to the match play."

"Why don't you spear yourself a crumb?" I asked, waving a hand at the room-service setup. "Plenty here for two."

Patterson accepted a French fry.

I crosshatched the steak into cubes. "Take the fork," I said. "I'm used to eating off the knife blade. Do it all the time."

"What happened?" he asked.

"Maybe your partner would like some of this," I said. "Why don't you go call him in from the car?"

"No partner, economy drive, one-man patrols," said Patterson. "What are you stalling around about?"

Well, I would have liked to shoo him away long enough to usher Nelda out of earshot.

"Let's eat up while the warmth lingers," I said. "And then sit in your car so you miss no radio calls maybe."

"Here I almost made the mistake of liking you."

"I don't care much to talk about it," I said. "I swam out there, I got back without actually drowning. I didn't do anything heroic, or save a life, and I would just as soon forget the whole thing. At least during mealtimes."

"Was there any life left to save?" said Officer Pat Patterson.

It was the way he sprung it on me. I stared at him, made busy mouth motions to show why I didn't answer.

"You heard me," he said, "and the steak isn't *that* tough."

I swallowed. "You heard me, too," I said. "I'm only the Courthouse Kid, and the coroner's office is up on the second floor. Where I come from, it takes an M.D. to sign the certificate."

"Where you come from," Patterson said, "do they know a live man when they see one?"

"Depends."

"On what?"

"On does he show any signs of it."

"Did Bob Crossway show any signs of it?"

"Not that I noticed."

Patterson stuck the cap back on his head, satisfied he'd pinned me down and got what he wanted. I didn't feel too bad, either, as at least I'd found out what it was he wanted.

"Mind if I ask you a question now?" I said.

"You can *ask*."

"It's how did you know to look for me here?"

"Very simple," said Officer Patterson. "I checked with the girl at the Surf Club if they had you registered there. Police work is mostly asking different people questions until you get honest answers."

If he'd been to the Club, he must already have asked Steve Gage the same question. "I pity anybody that gives you dishonest answers," I played up.

"You can say that again."

It sounded as if Gage had claimed we had Bob Crossway alive on that tube when we started the trip ashore. But why would he?

"Goodnight to you," I bade as he left. Then I headed for the bathroom to say the same to Nelda.

She was a sight, a bead of moisture on every hair of the mink, the wave out of her own hair, the black number dripping enough water to fill her shoes if her shoes would have held water.

It seemed when I took that steam shower, I should have switched on a concealed fan—Nelda politely explained this to me while I dug in the suitcase and found a flannel robe to wrap her in before pushing her out into the night. Which I did a bare five minutes before H. H. Crossway arrived.

EIGHT

THE OLDER FARMFOLK around Milquevais still follow the custom of holding wakes. They have the casket set up on sawhorses in the parlor, candlelight flickering on the departed's face.

The neighbors sit with the bereaved family, and there isn't much weeping—mostly small talk about crops and drinking coffee or maybe hard cider until it's time to morning-milk the cows.

In a sense, a wake for Bob Crossway was held at Chaparral House that night. But I doubt if such a fancy entered H. H. Crossway's thinking.

He came in the back way, nothing out there but vacant footage which the Texan probably intended to develop when the next gusher spouted.

Mr. Crossway did not act like a person sneaking in by the vacant lot and backdoor route, however. He created the appearance of the chairman of the board stepping from the private elevator into the directors' conference room. He wore a business-like expression and a dark business suit and had a fresh-lighted cigar in his teeth, even a briefcase at his side.

I started to say how sorry I was . . .

"It happened," he said. "It cannot be undone. The situation has changed, and we must reorient our thinking accordingly."

Was this the same man whose heart had bled on a sleeve a few hours ago? Well, you can't tell. The farmfolks back home don't necessarily mean all that free and easy chit-chat about the corn borer and the hog cholera . . .

"The unforeseen has occurred. Certain measures which appeared adequate in the past must be revised in the light of the present emergency."

As a reporter, I have to attend the annual cheese company meetings, and one year the plant lost money, and the executive secretary made this same kind of speech. They fired him, and he knew they would, which just goes to prove that under pressure the corporation chieftains run true to their type.

"Speaking frankly, Svederup, I wasn't entirely frank with you this afternoon. At that time, my objectives appeared attainable by a limited deployment falling somewhat short of a total commitment on my part. Do I make myself clear?"

"Yes," I said. "You had something up your sleeve."

His old denim eyes faded a bit more.

I didn't mean to hurt his feelings, either. It's just that newspaper reporters run true to their type, too. Even the small-town ones—especially the small-town ones, as they know personally the people who hang themselves from barn rafters and get killed driving home drunk from the Saturday night dance. You have to be hard-boiled or you go nuts.

"I admit," said the old man, "I envisioned an operation in which you, by cultivating Robert's confidence, could obtain and impart to me a few facts without necessarily evaluating their significance."

There was a gulf between the editorial office and the news room, which I felt had to be bridged. "I was to be the monkey," I said.

"Supposed to pass the hot chestnut without knowing what I had my paws on?"

H. H. C. looked as if one of his roses had unexpectedly thorned him. But he became a little more human.

"No reflection on you, young man," he said. "I haven't openly discussed this matter with my attorneys—or anyone else—not even Nelda, except in the most general terms."

"Only enough to kind of whet her curiosity," I said.

He didn't much like that.

"You are speaking of my daughter-in-law," the old boy said, as if she was of the royal line. In fact, there are some old-timers in the Crossway newspaper empire who claim the initials H. H. stand for "His Highness"!

"The nearest thing to being actually of my own flesh and blood," he went on.

"I didn't bring up her name," I said.

"Well," he said, "I wouldn't have either. Except before going any further with this, I must pledge you to secrecy. I ask you not to repeat what I say to anyone, including Nelda."

"Okay."

"She may try to pump you," he said.

"I'm a deep well," I said.

"Don't misunderstand me," he said. "I am fond of my daughter-in-law. In fact, when I disinherited Robert, I made Nelda my principal beneficiary."

"Big table stakes," I said.

"What?"

"Poker-playing expression," I said.

"Nelda doesn't gamble," he said. "She wouldn't fritter away my estate. Indeed, she might well develop into a principal figure in the newspaper world, as few other women have done."

"Without having her figure to start with."

"She's attractive," the old man said. "She might take it into her head to remarry."

He removed his cigar from his mouth and made an ash deposit in a metate tray.

"La Jolla has changed," he said.

"Every place," I said.

"Different class of people around. You used to know where the money came from. There were soap fortunes, dime store fortunes, meat packer fortunes. You could look them up in Dunn and Bradstreet." He worried visibly.

"Well," he went on, "we have a class of relatively young men nowadays riding around in Jaguars, floating around on yachts, and God knows where they get it. They seem to be influence peddlers, arrangers, five-per-centers who know somebody in Washington and somebody else in Sacramento."

"Nice work if you can get it."

"They don't work," said H. H. Crossway. "I made mine the hard way, and I would hate to leave everything to Nelda. And then have *her* die, and the fortune go to one of those operators."

I nodded intelligently.

"There are always worthy causes," I said.

"I would rather leave it to my own flesh and blood," he said.

"You might try naming the Billy Graham after an eligible young lady."

He scowled and sprung it on me abruptly. "Robert seems to have had a romance in *his* life. An involvement or mèsalliance or contretemps with a woman."

"So what?"

"There seems to have been a child," the old man said, "which, however illegitimate, is now the last of my line."

"So what is your problem? You leave your money to Bob's kid . . ."

The faded denim eyes under the grizzled brows regarded me glumly. "I would first have to find the woman and her child," he said.

"Let your intentions be known, and no doubt both will come forward."

"No doubt," said H. H. Crossway. "No doubt dozens and scores of unwed mothers would come forward with illegitimate children of both sexes and all ages if I advertised I was about to bequeath five million dollars to the most plausible claimant."

He jarred me. "You don't seem to know much about this," I said.

"Only what Robert himself told me."

He returned to his cigar for a while.

"I told you about the anniversary dinners," he resumed. "At the last, I got Robert into my study and tried to have a heart-to-heart talk with him. I said if he were a father he would better understand my feelings. He replied that he *was* a father, and he had no intention of dominating his child's life, and he went on to accuse me of being a power-lusting tyrant with an Almighty God complex who'd managed to rubber-stamp Junior in his own image and was trying to do the same to him. But we don't have to go into all that. . . ."

He sought some more comfort from his cigar.

"How long have you known?" I said.

"Little over a month."

"What have you done about it?"

"It took me a few weeks to get over the shock of the thing," he said. "I'm a man of old-fashioned moral ideas."

"Times change," I said.

"I can understand Robert having an affair," he said, "but I can't understand his fathering a bastard and letting it grow up wild. I told him so."

That must have helped a lot.

"It took me a while to realize the child in question was, after all, my grandchild. And I got to thinking of *you*."

"Why me?"

"It wouldn't have done any good to set a professional detective on Robert; he'd have seen through anything like that. And also, as I explained, I hoped you could turn up a clue to the mother and child without sensing the significance."

"You want my advice?" I said. "Hire a good one now."

"The best of them can't be trusted. They're all bedroom peepers and might palm off any floosie and her brat on me. Do it for a cut of my money." He had an eye out for booby traps. And for buzz saws, too.

"Might hurry me along to get the cut faster." I guess at a wake you always wonder who'll be next.

He put down the cigar, its moist end frayed from chewing. Then he stood up. "I want you to try. You're honest—too damned pointedly so to go down easily. But honest. Some of Robert's associates *must* know, and I'm counting on you to find my grandchild."

Meeting dismissed.

What could I say? It was partly, maybe mostly, my fault that Bob drowned. Looked at that way, I had a duty. . . .

H. H. C. was on his way out the back door.

"You forgot your briefcase," I said.

"Brought it for you. There's material in there that his Aunt Debby saved. It may help you get a line on Bob."

I watched him go, a man seeking to bestow five million dollars on a child that didn't even know the old boy existed.

NINE

THE CONTENTS of the briefcase were pathetic. Aunt Debby had treasured Bob's 1943 fifty-yard swimming plaque, his 1947 county fair blue ribbon won in the seashell collection class, his 1949 private school senior yearbook (he'd been nicknamed "Bugs," claimed water sports as his hobby, stated a life ambition of becoming a marine biologist). There were also letters from the headmaster trying to explain why a kid with such grades never got elected Class President, or even Class Secretary. "Lacks social orientation, deficient in personality adjustability."

I got the picture of a dogged, lonely, unpopular boy. Not the type to have developed into a fifty-romance chap. Most likely be a one-girl man, and the girl was probably of the Florrie Schultz stamp.

Bob had started to college in the fall of '49, and the score was pretty much as above until '51, when the briefcase record closed. Aunt Debby must have died then.

I pored over this stuff that night and picked up more from the morning San Diego *Union* that arrived with the iced papaya juice and eggs Benedict. The *Union* quoted the coroner as saying there'd be an autopsy to determine whether the cause of death was drowning or heart failure. An assemblyman was quoted as saying the dangerous sport of skin diving ought to be regulated by legislation.

I also learned Bob had graduated from college in '55 and had since been pursuing postgraduate studies at the Institute, shooting for Master's and Ph.D. degrees. Well, '49 to '55 spanned six years, and as college usually takes four, probably Bob had done his stint for Uncle Sam during that period. He might have gone overseas, maybe to Japan, and how would H. H. Crossway like an Asiatic grandchild?

I'd got that far when Officer Pat Patterson walked in—but not before I'd popped the briefcase under a divan cushion and myself on top of that cushion.

Officer Patterson was in an off-duty costume of black satin beach trunks and a chain suspending a religious medal from his neck. I wondered had he sneaked in posing as an early-hour pool-user.

"Toast?" I asked.

"I had breakfast," said he, taking some. "Look, if you're not a big-shot author, how do you afford the lap-of-luxury life?"

"Tell you. I got a little ol' forty-acre pasture that I decided to put in the soil bank so I could go see the world."

He half believed it. City people believe anything about the farm program.

"I understand you bought a stock of scuba equipment," Pat said. "Kelly girl told Mrs. Gage told Steve you're writing a book on skin diving."

"More of a magazine piece."

"My day off, so why don't you come along and let me introduce you to the local bugs and abs."

"Bugs and abs?"

"Lobster and abalone. You really don't know from nothin'."

I took him up on it, after submitting the imported Italian silk for valeting attentions.

Patterson drove a camp-trailer Ford truck; I followed in the wagon. Poster boy Don Diego was there again, pointing: "La Jolla Cove." I snapped the Leica at a very pretty scene of a beach washed clean by last night's tides, water sparkling blue-bright in the morning sun, and, out a ways, a cabin cruiser dropping a white-hull-and-brassworks reflection.

I pulled on my brand new wetsuit. Pat donned an old patched

one. We fitted on the belts with the detachable metal slugs ". . . to overcome our suits' buoyancy," Pat explained. We fitted on the fins, and he showed me about spitting on the glass face-plate to prevent fogging and helped me adjust the mask and insert the snorkel through the mask headband.

"Now we'll just paddle out—get you used to the leg action and the tube breathing." Off duty, he was as big a help to the tourist as Don Diego.

Only paddling around and staring down through the mask, I saw no abalone. After a while Pat surfaced, pulled out his snorkel mouthpiece, and called: "Ship ahoy!"

"Come aboard," a voice answered.

"Why don't we?" Pat said to me. "Del's a friend of mine, and this yacht is something to see."

We did. It was something to see. About the length of the Crossway swim pool. The owner said it could sleep eight and feed them out of the stainless steel galley.

His name was Del Bolling, and he had slept aboard in mandarin pajamas. He wore butterfly sunglasses that made it hard to guess his age, though it was probably thirty to forty.

"Svederup here is a big soil-banker from back east," Pat said casually.

Del Bolling's smile showed even, perfectly white teeth.

"I happen to know one of Ezra Benson's topdrawer men myself," he said. "A big-wheel crop-forecaster."

"How do crops look to him?" I said.

"There may be something about to move in soybeans," said Bolling, lowering his voice.

"Del dabbles in grain futures," Pat explained.

"Have you had an eye on the bean picture?" Del asked.

"Where I come from," I said, "you can't see 'em for the pesky weeds."

A kind of lull grew.

"Svederup comes from Minnesota," Pat said helpfully.

"The Golden Gophers," Del Bolling mused. "How do they look to you this year?"

"He dabbles in football pools," said Pat.

"I went to Iowa myself," I said. "School of creative writing."

"Svederup writes books and stuff," Pat offered.

Bolling surprised me. "Not my dish of tea," he said. "You have to do it yourself. No leaving the junior partner in charge while you dash off to Guaymas."

"Del dabbles in businesses where the other guys do the work," Pat contributed.

"I save my strength for recreational pursuits," said Del. "Oh, Ed, heat us up some Java."

Ed seemed to be the one-man crew of the svelte tub. A big,

tough-faced man in skivvies, tattooed on both arms, he served coffee from the galley. We sat down to drink under the mid-deck awning.

"Damn good coffee," said Pat.

"I did a little favor for the importer some years ago," said our host.

It'd been a long buildup, but Pat finally made the plunge. "Oh, say, Del, speaking of favors, how about a run up past the pier? Steve Gage told me he cut a lung off young Crossway, and we might take a look. Svederup ought to know within a few yards where it happened, hey?"

"Why?" said Del Bolling.

"The lung valve might have jammed, something like that."

Del didn't jump at it. But pretty soon Ed had upped anchor and was in the cockpit heading the cruiser up past the Surf and Racquet Club.

Back home, this would have been a job for the coroner and sheriff to supervise. It wouldn't have been left to a cop that had the day off and happened to know a guy who owned a boat.

"Were you raised here, Pat?" said I, looking at the scenery.

"Coronado. Why?"

"Live here?"

"Claremont, why?"

"Well, I thought if you were raised or lived here, you might know Bob Crossway personally and be taking a personal interest."

The comment brought out the Old Stone Age savage in Officer Patterson. Not in Bolling. I suspected he was laughing behind his dark-colored panes.

"I knew Bob slightly," he said. "Nelda, of course, completely charms me." There was more frosting on this cookie than I had at first thought.

"Dear Nelda," he mused. "In terror no doubt lest Dottie send flowers to the funeral."

"Who's Dottie?" I asked.

"Whose ain't she?" said the cop, trying to play it equally clever. The dark glasses flashed his way, then back to me.

"Dottie Vonn is a chanteuse more or less sporadically entertaining at Ye Olde Crowe's Neste. She's sporadic by nature, has her ups and downs, and in one of her downs is alleged to have tried to do the Dutch. Lovely girl, but depressive. It seems Bob Crossway saved her life."

"How?" said I.

"She cut her wrists and needed transfusions that she could not pay for, and Bob gallantly donated a few pints."

"Is that why Dottie might send flowers?" I said.

"That, and the fact she and Bob grew chummy. Found out they had more in common than just the same blood type, perchance."

The dark glasses flashed forward. "He didn't drown off Catalina, did he?"

The fact was, I had been assiduously making mental notes of all these windfall clues, if that's what they were, and we'd got 'way past the pier and under cliffs throwing blue-black shadows across the bows.

"Nobody said 'when,'" growled Ed, throwing me a soured look.

We had to turn back until I hazarded "when." It was pretty much a guess—yesterday's rocks were tided over now, and during the rescue attempt I naturally hadn't taken any sightings of landmarks.

"Coming along?" Pat said, slapping his fins past the stern observation chair.

"What's the technique?"

"Feet first—somersault once and you're under—kick on down." He led the way again.

It looked easy, and for a while *was* easy. I plummeted into the bracingly cool sea, felt a swell pass over my head, then doubled and did the head-down roll and started the fins threshing. I chased Pat's dive, could see the swirl patterns coming up through all that lovely peaceful green water.

Lake Milquevais was never like this. *Living* was never like this. Oh, I'd seen the movie shots, but in Cinemascope you can't *feel* it.

Thing was so wonderful I got the crazy idea Bob Crossway hadn't died such a bad death down here in the temple of the sea.

Then the pain stabbed me. Clobbered me. Sledge-hammered both sides of my head—blows that resounded on the brain.

I tried to take it, and I couldn't. Any more than I could tighten a vise that was cracking my skull. I arched up, kicked and clawed, and hit air a couple of feet from the boat's bow— a couple of feet from splitting my head on the keel.

I stared up, saw the name painted there: *Adventure II*.

It proved my eyeballs remained in place good enough to read. The brain behind them screwily remembered that *Adventure* had been the name of Captain Kidd's vessel.

A pair of butterfly sunglasses flashed over the bowrail.

"Something wrong?" As I couldn't read lips, I still had my hearing, too.

"Eardrums," I said.

"Swallow, cough, sneeze," said Del. "Clears the middle ear passages, you know."

It worked.

I dived again, only somehow the watery wonder-world no longer seemed quite so wonderful—just as the forest primeval loses some of its picnic appeal when those cute arbors of pretty leaves contain poison oak.

We prowled a while before we found the spot. Pat found it, actually. I dived beside him for a look.

The ocean floor here struck me as a continuation of the shore rock, possibly aeons before a solid ledge formation that an ancient earthquake had buckled and broken apart, leaving tilted, slippery slabs festooned with sea anemones and cucumbers and populated with little darting fish.

He groped and squeezed shoulders side by side up to a double fold in the slabs, a kind of crazily upsidedown V forming the mouth of a cavern God knows how deep.

The metal cylinder of the lung lay right at our feet, harness slashed, one of the breathing tubes curled over the pressure-gauge clockface. If it'd been a clock, its one hand would have been pointing to one o'clock.

We had to kneel, taking turns to peer into the cave. I was able to make out the shape of one fin in there, and an arbalete that had a diver's weight belt dropped across it.

We climbed back aboard the *Adventure II* and flopped on the deck, pretty well pooped. Pat, though, still had the breath to talk.

"Okay, now we know. Bob's bass took off into the nearest hole, the way a hurt fish will. And what Bob did was hook the arbalete line onto the tube, and go down, and follow Mr. Bass into the sea cave."

"Why didn't he just pull the fish out?" I managed.

"He'd have pulled the spearhead loose and lost a wounded bass. He thought he could crawl in and punch home another arbalete shot. The gun lay cocked, inside the cave."

He didn't have to tell me the gun was cocked. He told it for Del Bolling, sprawled in the observation chair over our heads. And I also noticed Ed picking up the coffee cups under the awning and not missing a word.

"Evidently the fish bolted out, and there was poor Bob messed up and tangled in the line that must have snagged farther back in the cave. Caught so he couldn't get out, and couldn't signal Steve with the fouled line."

There had been no Steve above to signal. . . .

"The lung gauge tells the story," Pat said. "Bob had been diving an hour and from the gauge could have lasted only another five, ten minutes."

"Could he *see* the gauge?" I said.

"Didn't have to. That's a demand type of lung valve, lets you know when the air's about gone." The cop's face had on a pitying, New Stone Age grimace. "Imagine a human being thirty to forty feet down and his air supply almost used up. . . ."

"Spare us all that," said Del rather edgily.

"It's the point. Bob had his choice. Play the waiting and praying game, lie there in that damned hole *hoping* Steve might guess something was wrong. Or else try to fight himself free of the tangle. Some choice, huh?"

Pat made you feel he'd watched it all happen.

"Bob panicked, smashed his face-plate as he struggled, lost consciousness and lost his lung mouthpiece. . . ."

Del Bolling leaned toward Pat, and it gave me a peek at the eyes behind his black cheaters. They were very flat, very pale, very remote.

"Just tell me," he said, "was Bob dead or alive when Steve got to him?"

Something in his voice made me wonder, *Did he dabble in cops, too?*

"Dead, absolutely," said Officer Patterson. "If he'd been alive and conscious, he'd have gone on sucking to the last drop of lung air."

This satisfied the *Adventure II*'s skipper. Me, I had a different idea from what I'd seen on the sea floor. An idea like the lonesome mosquito that buzzes around your pillow at night, making passes until you've got to turn on the lights and hunt it down.

TEN

A SCOPOPHILIAC is a Peeping Tom. I looked it up in the village public library. Actually, I called there in the interests of legal research. A volume entitled *California Law for Laymen* said the estate a testator could bequeath through an oral will was limited to one thousand dollars. It didn't seem enough to have frightened Nelda.

I still thought Nelda had been afraid last night, and the scopophiliac in me peeked into the situation and wondered if a man's dying declaration could acknowledge and legitimatize a child. But *Law for Laymen* left that point unanswered, so I had no real grounds to suspect Bob Crossway had been drowned *before* he could acknowledge and legitimatize a child.

Nelda might have done the deed, and Del Bolling might have had a dabbling hand in it. Was I stalking a deadly mosquito? Could the mosquito even now be stalking me?

Full of dangerous thoughts, I strolled along the village streets, noticing the high proportion of gift shops, women in shorts, sports cars of foreign makes. A window glittered with a display of tennis tournament trophies. A camera store placard advertised an Internation Photo Salon showing at the Art Center. Hardware bristled with the latest in patio barbecue equipment. Two bookstores in the one block offered the latest in light summer reading. Three exclusive milady's shops in the same block ravished the eye with creations that made Nelda's wardrobe seem conservative.

Under all this semitropical resort glamor must lie a sterner reality. I badly needed a Girl Scout to guide me through the crosswalks and cross-purposes.

I ambled on. I passed a flower shop where Dottie could have bought the funeral wreath. Another hardware front having a sale of scuba masks, spears, and suits—clearance before the legislature outlawed self-contained underwater breathing apparatus, maybe. Then men's wear that threw the Italian pure silk into the shade. Milady again, and next a regular junior department store of apparel for the kiddies.

Probably half the local population was juvenile. And Bob's kid didn't have to be local. There might be a hundred thousand in the San Diego area, a million in Southern California. People adopt them. You can't tell the difference.

I paused and checked the industrials on Briggs, Burton, and Leppner's board. Off 2.61. Railroads up .67, though. Well, we all have our confused, unsettled days.

It unsettled me some more to find Ava Gage alone in the travel agency. Her smile was as warm as yesterday's, although it seemed a little tired.

"I'm afraid La Jolla's giving you a rather sad welcome, Mr. Svederup. Usually it's such a bright, happy place—people come for a few weeks and stay the rest of their lives. . . ."

Which could be a short stay, at that.

"Healthy climate," I said. "A little damp in spots."

"No smog. Only about ten degrees' difference in mean annual winter and summer temperatures."

"Still, I suppose people catch colds occasionally," I remarked, glancing toward the hooded typewriter.

"Oh, Miss Kelly," Ava said. "I insisted on her taking the day off. This is a distressing, melancholy experience for her."

Ava looked me soberly full in the face as she said it, and from her eyes and voice and manner I gathered she meant to tell me something frankly and for my own good.

"Miss Kelly and Bob Crossway were, well . . ."

It hurt. Indeed, the sensation pressuring my skull resembled the undersea sledge-hammering.

"I didn't know," I gulped. The gulp didn't help much this time.

"Of course not, it happened so long ago," Ava Gage said softly as if to herself, and I couldn't see why she confided in me at all. Except, as H. H. Crossway remarked, people do tell me things. And sometimes I'd be happier if they didn't.

"She was only seventeen," Ava's gentle voice murmured, "and I'm quite sure Bob was her first love. And some of us never do entirely outgrow the first love with its dreams and illusions . . ."

Why should I have been so shaken?

I had known all along that Bob wasn't the type to consort with the Dottie Vonn character as described by Del Bolling. I'd told myself from the beginning it'd be someone of the nice, intelligent Florrie Schultz sort.

Kelly was a nice, intelligent girl, and why should I think her past romantic experience consisted of a summer of passing valve-lifters to a hot rod sweetheart? All the same, seventeen?

Still I knew too, it's the nice and decent and awfully young kids who are caught, while the older and more delinquent ones get away with it by knowing the ropes.

"Seventeen," I said. "That must have been five or six years back, at least."

"The summer of '50," Ava Gage said. "Naturally, she grew out of it. But not to the extent of becoming really interested in any-one else, which always seemed to me rather a pity."

These wonderfully womanly women, I reflected, *often have a streak of matchmaker in them.*

"In other words," she said, "it would help Miss Kelly enor-mously just at this time to meet some rather gay and even ebul-lient boy. Particularly if he happened to be sympathetic enough to understand if she proved a bit moody and not inclined to make dates. Who'd snap her out of a dreary spell, and won't be hurt, and wouldn't hurt her."

I said I just stopped by to look over the postcards, and I bought some dime-a-piece views of the coves and the caves, as I owed Florrie Schultz that much attention for emptying my mailbox of the rejected manuscripts during my vacation.

So I went out, and who should I run into but Steve Gage. He happened along the sidewalk just then to borrow the use of his wife's car.

"How's the writing coming along?" he asked.

"I'm distracted from it," I said.

"You're in the wrong atmosphere. Nobody could possibly ac-complish anything creative at Chaparral House. You need a quiet bachelor apartment where you could be alone with your Muse."

"Know of any such?"

"Hop in," said Steve.

He drove down onto Coast Boulevard near the Cove. The white brick and geranium window-boxed building curved to make the most of a sloping, pie-wedge lot. It had a charm without arti-ness that sold me even before we walked across the sidewalk and up the inner walk.

A small, very discreet sign screwed to the wall said: "Casa Luna Vista. Day, Week, Monthly Rates." There appeared to be eight units, each with a separate entrance.

"All permanent tenants," Steve said, fishing along the top of the sign and finding a key concealed there. "Two hundred a month, preposterously little in this location. Sun all day and a step to the beach."

We went in.

It was terrific. The apartment had a red brick wood-burning fireplace, colonial-scenes wallpaper, ocean-view windows that didn't try to let the ocean in, comfortable furniture that was neither too modern nor too antique. It had a common-sense kitchen, not one of those space-saving house-trailer kind of deals, full-size gas stove and big refrigerator. The bathtub was one a grown man could get into. There were two bedrooms, one of them fitted up as a working study—desk, electric typewriter, shelves of reference books.

It looked livable, and lived-in, and in fact had pipes on the mantel, clothes in the closets, a paper sandwich in the typewriter.

Finally, Steve broke the news. "This is Bob's place."

I switched from staring at the apartment to staring at him. He wore a quiet, businesslike air. "That's the explanation of the ridiculously low rent. Bob cared very little about money. He had no investment, as he inherited the building from his aunt. He'd a snug spot to live here and a modest income."

"Fourteen hundred a month," I said.

"Well, in La Jolla . . ."

So I wondered what his standards were.

"A first trust deed mortgage came with it, and later Bob put on a small second trust deed, and there were my management commissions. I would have boosted the ante, but he preferred quiet, permanent tenants."

He watched my face.

"Don't you like it?"

"I just can't figure it."

"The biggest homes in town are mortgaged to the top of their TV antennas," Steve said. "The rich pay four, five per cent for the other man's money. They use their own to get into and out of the stock market and so on. Question of quick cash when needed. I know of an operator who dabbled in grain futures, and ran a few thousand bucks up into around fifty grand. That's the way the money is made."

"Small world," I said. I hadn't been puzzling over the mortgage feature. "I myself just met a grain futures dabbler."

"You bump into it all the time here," said Steve.

"Still, it isn't such a small world you would have to rent this apartment to me, of all people."

"You wouldn't stay long," Steve said. "You'll write your piece and move on. I don't want a long-term lease here, because God knows what the Crossways will do. Sell it, knock it down, put up something twice as tall."

There was that.

"I don't want the average transient in here, either. You rent to a couple, they invite six to eight friends from Tucson or wherever it is, split the rent among the gang that's sleeping, slobbering, throwing wild parties all over the place." He told me some stories that proved the point.

"We'll move Bob's things out, of course," he said. "Leave you the electric machine in there and the books. I'm sure you'd treat 'em right, and Bob did so much of his work here you'll find quite a library on the undersea subject you're writing about."

There had to be a catch to it.

There was. He told me outside, after replacing the key.

"Didn't I mention something about a canceled appointment yesterday?" he asked.

"Yuh . . ."

"My *mistake. I thought* I had an appointment with Del Bolling yesterday. He didn't show up, and I supposed he'd canceled out on me, but he told me this morning he *thought* it was for *this* afternoon."

"Oh."

"*His* mistake I'm sure, but no use raising the issue at the inquest. If there is an inquest."

"I'll think it over," I said. "The apartment, I mean."

"Where can I drop you?"

I said I'd walk; I had to mail some postcards at the post office, anyway.

I walked around the block, helped myself to the key, and unlocked Bob Crossway's front door. Because you can never tell where a mosquito might alight. Because if Bob had been leading a double life, the apartment seemed a likely place to seek the traces of it.

I had ideas like a girl using the separate entrance, nighties tucked away in a closet, or maybe a ribbon-tied sheaf of love letters.

What I found was neither lacy nor sentimental. There were built-in drawers in the study, and in one Bob Crossway had dropped the flashlight he always intended to buy batteries for, and the lighter lacking a flint, the tennis balls that must have been good for another set several years past, the Xmas door wreath, and along with the rest, an old battered wallet.

Who can resist looking into old wallets? They might even contain money.

This one contained a college health insurance card which expired June, 1953, a public library card of the same vintage, a Pullman berth stub of the Los Angeles to Las Vegas run, and a snapshot of Bob and a girl and a toddler.

The girl wasn't anyone I recognized, and wasn't the Florrie Schultz sort at all. Even with falsies Florrie could never have looked like that.

The girl wore what I took to be toreador pants, and a very transparent but long-sleeved blouse, and had been caught looking squarely at the camera.

The toddler had been caught blinking in the sunshine and wore curls and a jumper suit which would have fitted either boy or girl of that age.

Bob wore a light-colored, probably Palm Beach suit and had been staring down at the child when the shutter clicked.

It encouraged me to look up Kelly in the local directory, the La Jolla one, with the local merchants' advertising and local street map and all the local residents over eighteen years of age.

Kelly, Mrs. P. T., widow, was followed by *Kelly, Clara, steno., Gage Trv. Srv.*

They answered in the same, the old woman first and next Kelly.

"Information?" I said.

"Oh, you," she said.

"I wondered if you knew of a fun place to eat lunch?"

"I know of a quaint drive-in down in Pacific Beach."

"Would you risk eating there yourself?" I talked her into it.

She and her mother lived down near the high school, on a street which still had the trolley-car tracks in the pavement and had comfortable front-porched houses in the big yards.

It wasn't an exotic part of the village; in fact, it reminded me of Milquevais. Kelly led me around to the back porch and introduced me to her mother. It was the kind of glassed-in back porch we have back home, and Mrs. Kelly reminded me of the women back home who sit in these porches and shell the garden peas. Mrs. Kelly was a smallish woman, blue-eyed Irish with black hair turning gray.

"Can you find Pacific Beach?" Kelly asked as we started off.

"I can always stop and ask Don Diego," I said. "How about that guy?"

Kelly told me the Don was the central figure of the big annual Fiesta during which San Diegans grew beards and wore historical Mexican costumes and had pageants.

So I told her about Milquevais Cheese Day, for which we grew beards and wore pioneer costumes and roped off Main Street for the parade. I explained that I worked on a Crossway paper back there and had had some of my stuff featured in thirty-eight Crossway papers.

We got along fine until we were parked at the drive-in and ordered our double-burgers and malted milks. I told her at that point that Mr. Crossway had put me on a kind of special assignment.

"You know," I said, "a lot of leaders of industry and titans of commerce are proud of their life accomplishments, and they sometimes hire talented young writers to prepare family biographies to be privately printed and circulated among their friends."

It didn't go down so good. Kelly's toast-brown eyes flashed me the kind of look she'd given me from the front of the car up there on the hill.

"I thought you were writing about scuba," she said.

"Well," I said, "it's a *family* biography. Mr. Crossway and Junior and Nelda are going to be in it, and I thought Bob should be, too. I wanted to get a line on his interests and scientific accomplishments and any other colorful material in his life." The trouble was, I had to get down to brass tacks and show her the snapshot.

"A writer of biographies has to dig through the old swimming trophies and county fair ribbons and school yearbooks in his search for human interest data," I said. "And, anyway, I ran onto *this*."

She didn't gasp or change color over the snapshot.

"That's Bob, isn't it?" I asked.

"Yes, it's Bob."

"Who's the girl?"

"I haven't the faintest."

Okay. She didn't know. No use to keep harping away on her heart strings already stretched too taut by Bob Crossway's death.

Kelly went on examining the snapshot, however. "The child," she volunteered, "I don't know him, either."

It came as a blow.

"How do you know it's a *him*, Kelly?" I asked.

"That's a boy, is all. You'd know"—and did I catch a hint of wry bitterness in her tone?—"if you'd baby-sat for your pin money as I did."

Well, I looked at her, this Kelly, this pretty girl with the delectable legs who'd been raised by a widowed mother living on a middle-class street. Who'd baby-sat for her pin money. I wondered how it all looked to a seventeen-year-old girl who'd grown up surrounded by the semitropical glamor of a resort town full of celebrities, full of people who dabbled in stocks and grain futures, full of old respected rich in palatial hilltop homes and of fast-buck new rich in foreign cars and cabin cruisers.

You bumped into it all the time, Steve Gage said. And mustn't some of it rub off on you? She'd been in love with the younger son of one of the thirty-five millionaires, Ava Gage said, and the possibilities frightened me.

I thought of Bob Crossway dying on the ocean floor for five million and one reasons. Five million dollars and one child that Kelly said was a boy.

What if she wasn't guessing, but *knew?* Then the mosquito I imagined buzzing on my trail could be stalking Kelly—to shut her up! I damned near yelled at her that she was in danger. Only, if I were wrong, I'd be an utter fool. And if I were right, to start yelling things I couldn't prove would make me a worse fool. It would send Kelly to the police if she believed me, and start a commotion that'd tip off the killer. So if I talked now, it'd be like trying to sneak up on Canadian Jones in a sputtering outboard with women and children along and in the line of fire. So I said, "Forget it. We'll eat."

The carhop had just come along to install the door-hung trays and serve the burgers and shakes.

"No," said Kelly, "I want to tell you what I think of you, Ken Svederup."

She said it with a smile. It was a friendly smile, and her voice picked its way trying not to hurt my feelings.

"I do believe, Ken, you're from your quiet, homey Milquevais. I imagine you're a good reporter, spell the names right, know your facts, and don't fall for the local, dirty-minded, mean-minded gossip. It happens, though, La Jolla is *different*. You're new here, and bewildered by the dash and glitter and sophistication. I see you as a barefoot country boy dazzled by your first glimpse of a three-ring circus, thrilled by the elephants and acrobats and calliope. And perhaps," grimly, now, "the beautiful bareback rider has smiled at you, too."

The words rang in my ears like a playback of my own forebodings concerning Kelly herself. Except I knew she was wrong about me, and wrong about Nelda's role if she meant Nelda.

"Picture speaks for itself, Kelly," I said.

I reached across her knees, under her tray, to the glove compartment. I carry an accessory telefoto lens for the Leica. It makes a usable magnifying glass. The kid's face swam up big on the snapshot, I had to admit, with boylike features. "He even has the Crossway granite chin," I said.

"Pictures can be faked."

"Pasted together and rephotographed," I said. "But then you get mistakes like eleven o'clock shadows on one face and two o'clock on another."

The shadows on this picture were uniform.

"Or," I said, "there are finer points. Because of different camera, different film grades, the variation between summer and winter light, resulting in different shutter speeds and lens stops so you have different depths of field, Kelly!"

"Greek to me."

"I mean, here the sharpness of focus is uniform. Bob's near shoulder and the child both in the same plane and both slightly fuzzy. Bob's face and the girl's both sharp."

The snapshot passed every test I could think of.

Kelly, now, became a sobered, earnest young woman. "What that picture implies," she said, "isn't and can't be true."

"But toreador pants? When were they the rage?"

"They aren't toreador, and four or five years ago."

"So four or five years ago, the child was a year and a half to two years old approximately."

"She might be wearing the year before's clothes."

"Anyway," I said, "during the summer of '50 didn't Bob donate blood to a certain Dottie Vonn?"

Kelly gave every appearance of trying to place the name.

"He may have," she said, "because Bob was a professional blood donor. His brother had died in Korea, and Mr. Crossway wanted Bob to drop marine biology and go into the family newspaper business. They quarreled, and Bob's allowance was cut off. In order to get money to go back to college the next fall, Bob worked at jobs like the Del Mar track, and sold blood for the $15 fee. I know all this, because he lived with us and shared Pete's room."

"Pete?"

"My brother."

"Oh."

"Pete and Bob were the same age and roomed together at college, took the same classes, worked at the same part-time jobs. . . ."

Of course, big brothers don't tell kid sisters all they know.

"Pete," I said, "sounds like a chap I'd like to meet."

"Any time you visit Woods Hole."

"Where?"

"It's an oceanographical research station located on Cape Cod," said Kelly.

Woods Hole sounded a little too far off. So I took Kelly home and turned around and followed Don Diego's directions into San Diego.

ELEVEN

BACK HOME, this would have been the easy step. A matter of adding nine months onto the summer of '50, after which the Courthouse Kid would have looked over the spring, '51, register of births, making a rundown of the mothers' maiden names.

By the time I'd passed through Pacific Beach and Mission Beach to the old amusement park roller-coaster, and across the Mission Bay resort development, and in past the cars parked around the Convair plants, I knew that it'd involve too much card-checking. And out here they wouldn't give me the run of the fileroom, anyway.

Back home, I could've used the *Globe*'s job press. Here, I found a dime store that printed while-you-wait cards.

Kenneth M. Svederup, Claims Auditor, Chaparral Insurance Company, and the hotel phone number. One of these I bestowed upon a middle-aged lady employee in the bureau of vital statistics record office.

The case involved some kids slightly injured in a subdivision excavation project, I said, and before compensating the parents the company wished to ascertain they actually were the parents because sometimes a divorced husband has been known to institute separate proceedings on grounds of being the affected juvenile's actual support.

The names? she inquired.

"Mr. and Mrs. Robert Crossway," I said, because there might have been a secret wedding, or the unwed mother might have assumed Bob's name.

The clerk looked as if she half-recalled seeing or hearing the name somewhere.

"Mrs. Dottie or Dorothy Vonn, a divorcee," I said, although, of course, that might have been just a stage name and Dottie was legally something like Von Beufieldendifer for all I knew.

"Mrs. Clara Kelly, a widow," I said, because even though I didn't think so, no reporter worth his salt can gloss over the involvement of someone he personally likes.

"You don't know the birth dates," the clerk said resignedly.

"They would all have been in '51; they are all kids the same age."

There were no birth certificates except those of half a dozen wrong Kellys.

"They might all have been born some place else," the clerk said. "Thousands and thousands of families move in here every year."

Yes, and unmarried girls go away to places like Los Angeles and Minneapolis and where-not to have their babies. It could have happened someplace else, and probably did.

"Oh, wait, here's another," I said. "Brad Gage, son of Mr. and Mrs. Stephen Gage." Because little Brad was about the suitable age, and I know of cases around Milquevais where the kind-hearted lady adopted the hired girl's trouble.

Nothing to it, though. It said on the card Ava had borne Bradley (that was her maiden family name) on Columbus Day, 1951, right in the hometown Scripps Hospital with a Dr. Hobleigh as the attending physician.

I could think of nothing better to do than drop in for a beer at Ye Olde Crowe's Neste.

The Neste was reached by following Harbor Drive. And I felt almost like a Russian spy, with a Leica and a telefoto lens in the car, driving past a big aircraft assembly plant on the right, and the airfield beyond, and on the left San Diego harbor stuffed full of about half the U. S. Navy. And after that, an end-piece of a naval training center with recruits practicing how to control fire damage—ready for me if I had thrown a bomb, which I could have easily.

Then if I had thrown it, I would only have hit Shelter Island

and merely killed off some of the rich taxpayers lounging about
the Kona Kai Club. I knew all about them, thanks to the Florrie
Schultz system of advance research. Ye Olde Crowe's Neste I re-
searched out by my own system of looking for the Neon signs.

I headed in where a pier stuck out into the bay and unsaddled
in a parking area reserved for the owners and guests of a flock of
anchored yachts and cruisers. I didn't see *Adventure II* among
them. I walked back past a ship's-chandler establishment on the
corner which was equipped with a bench and a bus stop sign. Next
door to the chandler was a pizza place, and the door beyond
opened into Ye Olde Crowe's Neste.

It resembled a fine old London coffee-house in which the mer-
chant princes of the grand old East India Company might have
lounged and gazed through lead-paned windows at the shipping
on the Thames. *These* windows, of course, overlooked the pier
and the yacht anchorage. The other walls were windowless, dark-
paneled, with pictures of clipper ships and a few exhibits of whaler
harpoons and of bones dissected from harpooned whales.

The elderly barman had a white walrus mustache not grown, I
felt sure, for the Fiesta. He stroked it as he gazed on the behind-
the-bar teevee screen on which a lovely Pantry Playhouse hostess
was encouraging a teen-age kid to show how he won the Balboa
Park yo-yo layoffs.

It wasn't as much of a false note as Ye Olde Crowe Neste's jukebox, however. I took a table facing the waterfront view. Yo-yo's
we have back home.

The barmaid followed my wake, a girl as buxomly built as the
figurehead lady on a clipper ship. "What'll it be, sir?" said she.

"You got something I could wash down with a tankard of
ale?" I said.

"Another ale," she said.

"I was thinking of a beef pie, slice of Stilton, something like
that."

"Mmm. I could get you a pizza from next door."

"Pizza what?"

"Please, sir," said she.

I explained I was a stranger in town. "From Texas," I said.

"Pizza is an Italian cheese pie, sort of," she said.

I ordered it, expecting a conversation piece. She returned from
next door with a plate at least twelve inches in diameter.

"That ought to last me until the first floor show starts," I said.

"Floor show? Here? Where'd you get that idea?"

"Word-of-mouth advertising," I said. "I overheard Dottie Vonn
was entertaining here."

"Dottie doesn't work here," the barmaid said. "If you're a bill
collector thinking of garnisheeing her salary, she doesn't get paid."

"Amateur?"

"Professional trying to get her hand in after retirement owing to illness," the barmaid said. "She's a friend of a friend of Mr. Crowe's. She drops in during the evening; it helps keep her in training."

She walked away. I waded into the pizza. If one Italian eats all that at a sitting, I don't know how he does it. Finally, however, I reached the other shore.

I signaled the barmaid and paid. "Here," I said, "kindly give Miss Vonn this," slipping her a dime-store print sample.

"Are you sure this is on the up-and-up?" the barmaid said.

"She doesn't have to ring the number unless she wants to ring the number," I said.

I drove back to La Jolla by way of Rosecrans Street and the Mission Bay causeway and stopped by to see if Steve Gage might be in his real estate and property management office. He wasn't. Tried the post office to see whether Florrie Schultz had forwarded any mail care of general delivery. She hadn't. I left the Chaparral House as the forwarding address, bought an afternoon newspaper, and drove back to Chaparral House.

The desk clerk cashed a traveler's check for me, and handed me a package. It contained my robe, which Nelda had returned without tarantulas in the pockets. And valet service had brought back the imported Italian pure silk masterpiece.

The afternoon paper said on page two that Robert Crossway had died by drowning, not heart failure.

I tried to call Steve. His telephone robot said he would return shortly and gave me thirty seconds to leave my message. I asked him to call me.

I read the rest of the paper. There was a lively 'round-town columnist on page twelve, so I gave him a ring.

"I have a cafe society tip for you," I said. "What well-known man-about-boats is dropping anchor at which lovely widow's La Jolla dock?"

"I know the answers. Del Bolling and Nelda Crossway," the columnist said. "The column noted it in connection with a Playhouse opening ten days ago, but thanks for confirming it."

I hung up and said, "Thank *you* for confirming it."

So I sat around and wondered whether I heard a mosquito or a buzz saw or just my imagination.

An hour and a half elapsed before the phone rang and a slightly tipsy feminine voice came through, "Mr. Sv'd'up?"

"Speaking," I said. "Miss Vonn, I presume?"

There seemed to be something wrong at the other end. She dropped the phone or something. "You all right?" I said.

"I'm a little drunk-y and scared-y. You aren't trying to sell me some insurance, are you?" she asked.

"It's in connection with Mr. Robert Crossway's death," I said.

"My God. Bob din't leave me some insurance, did he?"

"I could hardly discuss *that* over the phone with an unidentified voice."

"Well, I'm home right now. It's 1828 Dulcine Street, 'partment G. Like gee-whiz. It's an outside stairs. You come up, third door. Dulcine Street is only two blocks from Ye Olde Crowe's Neste." She sounded constrainedly sober now.

"I'm afraid it's rather far out of my way," I said.

"You want me to come to your office?"

"I'm afraid it's rather late for that."

"Tomorrow."

"Tied up tomorrow."

"My God," she said. "Can't you give me some idea?"

"Let me think. Look, I'm in La Jolla, out near the Surf Club. Why don't you take a cab and meet me at the Maritime Room and we'll discuss this over a bite. I'll take care of the cab part, of course."

"Shall we say the fashionable hour of eightish?" Dottie Vonn asked.

"Let's make it the business-like hour of seven," I said. "And as a matter of business, bring with you any available credentials tending to confirm any relationship you may have had with Robert Crossway."

Right after I hung up, the phone rang again. Steve. "Have you thought over that apartment?" he inquired.

"To the extent of wondering what Bob's family would think of rushing his stuff out and me in," I said.

"Oh, I talked with Mrs. Crossway, Jr., before talking to you."

"Her idea?" I said.

"The responsibility of packing Bob's things falls on her, and Nelda isn't one to put off doing a job. She'll have the place ready in a jiffy."

"She has a key?"

"She stopped by the office for a key, and that's how all this came up."

Nelda had a key? She could have planted the wallet in the study, but why would she?

"Ava is taking Brad to the movies, and you might like to drop in and eat with me at the Club."

"I'm eating there," I said, "with a young lady."

It'd got past eightish when Dottie Vonn disembarked from her cab. She was a brown-eyed blonde, blonder than I'd expected from the snapshot, and quite a bit drunker than I'd expected from our phone conversation. But quietly drunk—no staggering, no loud talk.

She was in a silver lame gown that was undoubtedly a professional entertainer's costume—no back to it and a seriously eroded front, but with dramatic full-length sleeves.

"Well," I asked, "would you prefer to sit facing the Maritime Room's enormous slab windows being rinsed by a high tide outside, or would you like to look across the dance floor at the fish murals behind the pianist's back?"

"You're welcome to the spray," she said. "I got a lifetime of it in my water ballet days."

"I could have guessed you were a swimmer."

"How?"

"They have such marvelously developed figures." This wasn't flattery; she deserved the compliment.

"I can't swim a stroke," Dottie Vonn said. "I vocalized on top of the fountain in the ballet tableau."

"Where?"

"Vegas," she said, "and believe me those desert nights get chilly for taking outdoor showers dressed just in glitter paint. Just thinking of it, I could use a little nip."

But I didn't want her any drunker. "I never mix the stuff with business," I said. "Suppose we settle for a warming consomme?"

We ordered it and the prime ribs *a jus*.

"So I'm Bob's ben—what do you call it?"

"I haven't said you were his beneficiary."

"Then what the hell is all this?"

"There might be another beneficiary, and it would still be necessary for you to answer certain questions. Clear up points only you can clear up."

I placed the snapshot on the tablecloth between us.

"Where'd you ever find that?" said Dottie. "Gee, those pants, did I look a fright. But it brings back memories."

"Your memories are what I need."

"I hardly know where to begin, though . . ."

"Why not when *it* began?"

The consomme had a steadying, sustaining effect. It did not make her any less drunk, but it did enable her to talk coherently and to the point. It seemingly had the further effect of lowering her inhibitions so she could talk frankly on the details that sober, inhibited people like to blur over.

"I was out of a job. Trying to make a living off the ponies at Del Mar. Well, tell you, I had a big losing streak. I got sick and blue, and the next thing I woke up in the hospital. The truth is, I'd let out a lot of blood that needed replacing and I couldn't pay for it.

"And," said Dottie looking down at the snapshot, "*he* came to the rescue."

"A lucky coincidence you were the same blood type."

"Were we?" said Dottie. "I thought they just took the blood out of the blood bank, and he guaranteed to make it good with the bank. Anyway, I was grateful."

"Naturally."

"So I thanked the kid. We had a few dates. Well, I found myself in the condition."

She did not try to put up a big emotional smoke screen about having been madly in love with Bob. I liked her for that.

"Okay, well, my agent landed me the water ballet job in Vegas. I didn't try to put the bee on Bob, either. I thought of him as a poor college student in no position to help out. Maybe he *would* have married me, and it looked to me in that case I'd wind up supporting the baby and putting Bob through college besides."

A pause while the bus boy removed the consomme cups.

"Anyway, actually, my idea was to drop the whole subject—if you know what I mean. And I realized Bob was too high-minded to go for *that*, and it's another reason I didn't tell him at the time."

The ribs arrived.

"Go ahead and hate me," said the brown-eyed blonde. "I've been hated and insulted and slapped around before. That was another reason."

An especially heavy wave sloshed on the Maritime Room glass. The dinner-jacketed and corsaged diners at the waterfront tables looked up with appreciative, interested smiles. They had all that thick, armor-plate glass between them and the tides and the night.

"Didn't you know Bob's family had money?" I said. "They might have helped you?"

Dottie hesitated.

"If they wouldn't help him, why would they help me? Bob was selling his blood and working summers at Del Mar track's parking lots."

She hesitated some more.

"I'll tell you," she said. "I happened on a magazine expose of the black market in babies. It claimed girls were getting their doctor and hospital bills and up to a thousand and two thousand dollars in cash. I figured it was better than paying some dirty crooked backstairs operator who might kill me besides."

Another wave thrilled the diners.

"So I quit the water ballet, went to work behind a twenty-one table, and was a little lucky at roulette, too. And signed in at the hospital as a Mrs. Smith, with the booty right there within reach."

She paused.

"Well, he was such a tiny little tyke, not strong, maybe on account of all I'd been through. Not the husky infant anybody would pay money for. It wasn't just maternal love on my part. I had him, so I took my little Jackpots home and pretended to be another Nevada divorcee staying on and supporting a kid by working behind the tables."

"You'd better eat, Miss Vonn."

"I don't have the appetite. . . ."

We have a few alcoholics back in Milquevais, and they don't have the appetite, either.

She talked on. "A girl has to stay *behind* the tables to do it, and I got to gambling, and a couple of years found me broke. I thought a letter to Bob in La Jolla might reach him. I had to borrow the three-cent stamp from the other girl we lived with."

"We?"

"Jackpots and me."

"Oh."

Dottie's brown eyes stared at the snapshot. "The other girl, she took that picture. The time Bob came there to Vegas."

"Did he acknowledge the child as his?" I said.

"Well, I needed a couple hundred bucks to tide me over, and he gave me the couple hundred."

"I mean in writing," I said.

"Well, he paid to support the child," said Dottie. "I didn't need it in writing whose kid Jackpots was. I needed the cash."

"Have you no proof of any kind?" I asked. "Checks, letters, birth certificate?"

A trayful of cocktails went by.

"I need a drink," she said. "The truth is, I lost the kid. I can't tell you that part without a drink first."

I called the waiter.

"A tourist driving through town didn't think kids might be playing in the street."

She was not crying, or trying to, or trying not to. She looked bad, and the waiter got the drink to her in a hurry.

"Well, I had losing streaks before and since, but that was the God damnedest."

The kid was dead, but had Bob ever known about that?

"So about this insurance thing," said Dottie. "Will the company pay *me* since Jackpots is out of the picture?"

She'd become suddenly a changed and toughened blonde with the fresh drink in her. Maybe she lied about the kid's death so she could collect the imaginary insurance.

"You will receive some money," I said, "if and when you prove the child was yours and was Bob's and is dead."

H. H. Crossway would just have to fork it up.

"I don't hand over any proof of anything to anybody," said Dottie Vonn, "until I see your promise in writing signed by somebody else than you. And I repeat, how much money?"

We have drunks back home who get hostile with one too many, and where isn't it true?

"There could be no money if you take this attitude," I said.

"I don't like guys who won't buy me drinks," said Dottie. She beckoned the waiter. The wrist appearing out of her dramatic long sleeve wore a thin-seamed scar line.

"*Garcon*, another little soupcon of the same. . . ."

The waiter looked dubious, but I nodded to him.

"What do you mean," I said, "signed by somebody else? Who else?" She probably wouldn't have told me, anyway, but just then I felt a light touch on my sleeve. There was a voice, too: "Hello, Ken." It was little Brad, with a paper sack in his hand and the smell of popcorn on his breath.

Steve and Ava were just inside the doorway. Ava was looking at Dottie. Dottie was sneering at me.

"Where's Kelly?" Brad said. "I thought you were stepping out with Kelly."

I managed to catch Steve's eye, and he started our way.

"What's your name?" the kid said to Dottie.

"Miss Vonn," I said. "Master Bradley Gage."

"You're pretty," Brad said acknowledging the introduction, "but Kelly's beautiful."

"Beddy-bye time, son," said Steve. "Excuse him, Miss——?"

"Vonn," said Brad. "She's drunk. Kelly doesn't drink. Mummy says . . ."

"Miss Vonn," said Steve, "would you care to dance?"

She would. They did. By that time, Ava had closed in and captured Brad.

"Well, Ken," she said, "you took the hint with a vengeance, didn't you?"

I had liked Ava tremendously from the start, and I still liked her, but it did seem to me she was working overzealously at mapping out itineraries of other people's lives.

"I'm going to tell Kelly," said Brad.

"There's nothing to tell, dear," said Ava. "Your mother is a sentimental woman who became emotionally upset over what was none of her business. Mr. Svederup is an imaginative young author who made a soap opera plot of it. Gracious! Miss Kelly has too much sense to make an issue of a strange man taking another girl to dinner." She smiled a tired, sad smile. "Oh, Ken, if it hadn't been so obviously the first pickup that came along . . ."

"She's picking up Daddy now," said Brad.

In fact, Dottie Vonn and Steve were leaving the far side of the dance floor.

"Excuse me," I said.

I caught up the snapshot, and caught up with the pair around the corner at the Maritime Room bar.

"Sure, I'll buy you a drink," Steve was saying. "We never punish the child in public, bad for his ego."

Maybe he had whirled Dottie away before she said something injurious to Brad's ego.

"Oh, Ken," he said. "Have you made your decision on that place of Bob's?"

"The wife and child await," I said.

"It must be costing you at least eighty dollars a day at Chaparral House."

Those were his words. He couldn't have said eight, and it didn't sound like eighteen.

"And a very few days of that would more than cover a month's rent of Bob's little apartment."

It gave me a notion of where Brad inherited a big mouth and the foot to put into it.

"Jesus, eighty bucks a day for a hotel room?" Dottie said.

"I am not in the royal bridal suite," I said. "In the annex to the boiler room."

"What's all this about a little apartment?" Dottie went on. "I'm interested in that myself."

"Better grab it now," Steve grinned to me. "I may show her the place tomorrow."

"Let's you and I go and look at it tonight—the night's young." Dottie snared a squat shot glass from the bar. "Excuse me, lover," she said to the nautical uniform at her elbow.

"Why, Del," said Steve.

It was Del Bolling in the white, gold-buttoned and gold-braided yachtsman's coat, and without the sunglasses I could hardly have recognized him. He now looked like an altogether ironic, intelligent, and blasé first-nighter.

He spoke first to Dottie. "Drowning grief in the cup that cheers, I see."

He had a white, gold-braided skipper's cap on the bar that he picked up and very smoothly held so that it shielded his face from Dottie, like John Daly on "What's My Line?" conferring behind a contestant's cheek.

"Dipso," he said to me. "Depressive phase. Reefs ahead," and he followed the cap around and stood next to Steve. "How would an Ensenada cruise strike you? I'm dropping down tomorrow. If you could be free . . ."

"Impossible," said Steve.

"Svederup?" said Del. "Very lovely bit of Mexican coast there. Unsurpassed sport fishing. The most wonderful skin diving anywhere, and you could learn more in a week end there than in a month of La Jolla."

Everybody wanted to help me out. Patterson, Steve Gage, Ava Gage, Don Diego, and now Del.

"Who's buying the next round?" said Dottie gaily.

"I couldn't," I replied to Del.

"Oh, loosen up," said Dottie. "We had our business talk."

"Where I come from," I said, "if one guy supplies the car, the other buys the gas. I couldn't afford to fuel your boat."

He stared. "You can't be serious," he said. "None of it could cost you one thin dime."

"Matter of principle with me."

"But I take writers and painters on these jaunts all the time. For the perfectly selfish reason that they make much more interesting companions than do the business types—not you, Steve, the high-pressure ones I go there to escape, to be precise."

Dottie grabbed my sleeve and looked up into my face. Her face showed she had got this far by a tortured, tortuous journey. "I lied to you before," she said. "My baby came too soon, and you can't blackmarket a premature kid. Buy me a drink and I will tell you the whole truth."

She began to cry, depressively.

The bartender noticeably noticed.

"Come, Miss Vonn," I said.

"One for the road," she pleaded.

"Let me handle this," said Del Bolling very quietly.

"I couldn't," I said.

"Dulcine Street is only steps from where I have the boat tied. On my way, no trouble at all."

"Matter of principle where I come from," I said. "A guy doesn't take out a girl and after she's stewed let some other guy have the job of seeing her safe home."

So I was the one that took Dottie back to Dulcine Street.

TWELVE

SEVERAL INCIDENTS occurred en route.

Dottie wanted to get out a couple of times and visit bars along the way. One of those times the car was moving, and I received slight facial scratches while subduing her with one hand while driving with the other.

The Dulcine Street place stood on a corner, a long, narrow white clapboard structure with doors opening on the sides upstairs onto a space-saving outside catwalk. Each door was lighted by a little dim bulb burning in a mail-order-house fixture screwed into the door frame. They have those same fixtures on the porches in Milquevais. Also the same horseshoe style of door-knockers.

Dottie didn't want to give me the key to Apartment G; she wanted to go to Ye Olde Crowe's Neste for a nightcap. She said so noisily—so much so that the door of Apartment H opened, and a woman put out her head and called, "Either you get to Alcoholics Anonymous, or one of these nights I will call the police."

I seized Dottie's purse, found the key, and rushed her inside.

"I got to go to the little girls' room," she said.

I looked around the apartment. It was a one-room-with-kitchenette deal, furnished by Sears Roebuck—I recognized some of the pieces—the tube-steel-legged divan that made a bed, the tube-steel-legged matching chair and footrest that could make a second bed. The portable TV and the travel-case record player came from somewhere else. Beyond a formica-topped table was a cooking area just large enough to contain a four-cubic-foot refrigerator, a thirty-inch electric stove, a stainless steel sink, and a telephone. Half a pot of coffee stood on the stove, and I switched up the juice. It boiled before Dottie came out of the little girls'.

She had been so quiet that I wondered if she had opened her wrist again. But what she had opened was a bottle, as I knew as soon as she came out. And the depressive phase had again changed into the antagonistic.

"Why don't you crank up your rattletrap covered wagon and go on home to your eighty-dollar-a-day boiler annex?" she said.

I did, because there was no talking to her in that mood.

It was a little hard to fall asleep, mulling over the events of the night's dinner. I felt that Dottie's story had been mostly true in the sense that something like what she said must have happened. She had been so careful to hold back the details about the child and the name of the woman who snapped the picture and the dates. Out-and-out liars supply the details to make the lie convincing.

Del Bolling knew Dottie, knew where she lived, probably knew the whole story, too. Or he could get it from her any time he wanted. True, he had made no effort to hide his acquaintance with Dottie; but then he had been just as frank about knowing Nelda.

No doubt about it, he was a smart cookie. I wondered if he had steered me toward Dottie, had planted the snapshot for me to find, and had been hanging around the Maritime Room to break things up if Dottie became too drunkenly talkative. Especially, I wondered about the Ensenada invitation.

I decided to telephone the Crossway residence. Maybe the servants had retired, because Nelda answered.

"I suppose you expect me to wake up Father Crossway," she said.

"You will do," I said. "I wondered when the services were."

"Why, day after tomorrow. Why do you ask?"

"A fellow invited me on a boat trip leaving tomorrow," I said, "but I guess under the circumstances I shouldn't."

"I don't see why not. It will be at the mortuary chapel, a very quiet service for the family and a few of Robert's colleagues from the Institute. You never knew him, and why should you feel obligated to attend?"

Which confirmed my idea that she wanted me to go.

Next I looked up Pat Patterson in the phone book, because on night duty the day off really means the night off.

"The police department have any plans of issuing a subpoena or warrant for me that you know of?" I asked him.

"Why should they?" the cop asked. "The whole thing was an

accident. I told you so, and the coroner made it official today.
What are you worrying about?"

"I'm invited on a boat ride to Ensenada, and I wouldn't want to
create the appearance of leaving U. S. soil a jump ahead of a subpoena or a warrant."

He thought a while. At least, he neither said anything nor hung
up.

Finally he came to a decision.

"Suppose I check and call you back before you do anything
definite."

Sleep came while waiting for him to call back. It was 2:30 A.M.
when the phone woke me up.

"Swer'up?"

It was Dottie's voice, sounding very "drunk-y" now and, I
thought, very "scared-y." There was also a lot of background noise
that sounded like it might have been Ernie Ford hollering "Cry,
Baby, Cry" or "Why, Baby, Why?" along with some other clatter-
bang.

"I foun' out who you are, *what* you are, who's paying you,"
Dottie said in a sullen, soured tone.

"Speak up a little louder, please, Miss Vonn."

"I did get the ten grand off Bob that time in Vegas," the
drunk-y, scared-y, sullen voice said. "I had it comin', and don't
think you're goin' to send me up for 'stortion, or somepin.'"

"Who have you been drinking with?" I asked. "Nothing to it,
but who told you?"

"You *or* the Crossways," she said, off on her own different wave
length.

"Where are you? I'll come right over and straighten this out."

"Want you to know what I think of *you*—lyin', stinkin' bastard.
Couldn' reshish tellin' you off 'fore I skipped—*shipped*—out."

"Dottie, I wouldn't deceive you. I never heard of any ten grand,
. . ." But the wire had gone dead.

I had known that foot-in-the-mouth yakking of Steve's about
the eighty-dollar hotel rate was going to cause trouble. She must
have got up onto a high plane of intoxication, which freed the
subconscious mind to interpret me as a Crossway undercover
agent.

I groped out of bed and fumbled into stretch socks, shirt, and
imported Italian pure silk.

On Mission Boulevard I ran into fog, at first just enough to
smoke up the windshield with film the wipers turned into smears.
The wagon's first owner had been a Model-T-minded man who
hadn't gone in for any of that pack of extras like jets to squirt on
the glass—said a man too lazy to clean his windshield could
hang a head out the window. I hung a head out the window.

The fog thickened. I got down onto the waterfront in a

closed-in world of mist and vague hulking storefronts and far-off mooing harbor horns. I missed Dulcine Street and never knew it until the word *PIZZA* dripped down among the other sinister visual effects. So I swung past the chandler's and into the parking lot.

A quiet lapping bespoke the presence of harbor waters. With eye-straining, I could make out the pier marching into the mist. The boat lights, if any, were obscured.

One question was, Where had Dottie phoned from, and one answer suggested Ye Olde Crowe's Neste as a source of background jukebox music.

I got out and picked a flashlight from the glove compartment and made my way past some other parked cars to the chandler's corner. I came onto a girl waiting on the bus bench. Maybe Dottie was decamping by bus, and I had arrived in time to intercept her.

There was a question about how seriously to take Dottie's threats of skipping or shipping out. We had a fellow back home that, every time he got a skinful, announced he was going to climb the water tower and sprinkle the whole town. The one time he ever tried it, we figured he must have reached the top—from the condition of the body, the unzippered fly, and the post-mortem empty bladder. It must have been the fog and the dark and the loneliness that put me in the mood to recall it.

This girl jumped from my flashlight when I played it on her, and she made a shot-slung of the purse in her fist, and circled to keep the bench between us. I wondered what fog, dark, and loneliness reminded her of. She was scared-y, all right, but she wasn't Dottie Vonn!

I continued on down under the pizza sign. Inside the shack the cold lights bathed the chairs upended onto the tables and a porter mopping the floor.

Ye Olde Crowe's Neste had a light burning, too, behind the bar. I rattled the door. No answer. I did seem to see a thread of cigarette smoke purling about, though it might have been fog beyond the lead-paned windows.

I retraced my steps and rattled the pizza palace's full-length glass door. The porter shook his head at me. I started hunting in my pocket for a dollar bill, and while I was doing it, a cold drop of condensed moisture from the neon dripped down my neck. I rattled the door again and spread a single against the glass.

The porter came over, but he didn't open up. "Man, we closed here," he said. "Can't you see, man?"

"What time did the joint next door close up?" I said.

"Two o'clock, that's the legal hour, man. Man, you can't buy no liquor this time a night."

"Didn't they have the jukebox blasting as late as two-thirty?" I asked.

He shook his head. And if he could hear me, he would certainly have heard Ernie Ford, if it was Ernie Ford.

The glass was so damp that the dollar bill stayed stuck, and I left it there and walked on through the foggy dark loneliness. This time I found Dulcine Street where I'd left it half a dozen hours before. The bulbs in the door frame fixtures had fog haloes; the hand railing was wet to the touch; and up on the catwalk moisture from the roof overhang dripped onto my neck.

Dottie's windows were dark with all the rest. I knocked gently. She might be sleeping it off. Then I risked the knocker—it made a hell of a racket.

A window of Apartment H raised, and the woman put out her head.

"Go home," she said. "Break it up, let decent people get their sleep."

"I'm sorry, madam," I said, "I guess we were a little noisy here tonight."

I could hear her breathing hard.

"With the record player and all," I said.

"Go home," she said. "Men like you ought to be arrested for getting girls like her in that condition."

I said nothing, for I had just noticed the big wet footprint. Somebody ahead of me had left it planted across the dry portion of the catwalk, pointed at Dottie's door. It occurred to me to test the knob. The door wasn't locked.

"Beat it," called Apartment H, "before I call the cops."

"Lady," I said, "if you hear one more peep, you just do that thing."

I pushed open Dottie's door and held it open so that the lady couldn't miss hearing the shot. But there wasn't any.

I reached inside the door jamb and switched up the lights. The place looked empty and reasonably tidy—no signs of a wild and boisterous party. No signs of anything much except one more wet footprint on the way to the cotton carpeting.

I looked into the bathroom, hoping anybody hiding in there would be just as timid and peace-loving as myself. Then I looked into the clothes closet. If Dottie had skipped or shipped, she had done so without troubling to pack her wardrobe.

It really seemed likely she was somewhere else, drinking and coming unstitched. There are drunks who call up their friends for sympathy, and other drunks who call up people they don't like and pick arguments, and still other drunks who telephone the police or the newspaper editor and make wild threats of doing themselves in.

Only Apartment H had heard something in here, and there was still the footprint business— Just the one set of footprints, because *my* feet hadn't been wet enough to leave tracks, and I had walked several blocks to get here.

So I had a look at the record player. "Why, Baby, Why?" was the record on the turntable. The coffee pot in the kitchen remained half full. In the stainless sink were partially melted ice cubes and the tray they had come from. I rattled the tray around in the sink, gently. It clatter-banged.

I switched off the lights and closed the door and headed for the waterfront. When I came to sand, I thumbed on the flashbeam. It was white sand, full of footprints. Farther out was darker, wetter sand left by the ebbing tide. The tide had been high around eight, and I walked a ways before I came to the footprints left after them.

They were deep when I found them. I might have been on the trail of a fat drunk who took short, staggering steps from having a load of hootch in him. Or it might have been the trail of just any man stumbling from carrying a load of just anything.

The footprints went right down to the edge of the wave-washes and might have continued right on out among the fog-shrouded cabin cruisers and yachts. There were no returning tracks—none that I saw, anyway. I hadn't so much time to look, though.

A bigger, brighter flashlight than mine smashed through the mist onto me, and a voice behind it yelled: "Hold it!" Or "Hold on!" or even, "Hold up!"

That kind of yell took me by surprise, and I acted on instinct and conditioned reflexes, and hurled my flashlight at the Voice's head.

I hadn't coolly reasoned that the light streaking toward his face would startle him into ducking or throwing up a warding arm, and so give me a split second to try out a dive-tackle.

It worked that way, though, and I cracked him across the knees. We both went down. I was on top of him, briefly. The feeling resembled being on top of a wild steer in a rodeo.

He seemed to be all knees and fists, and we rolled over. I was under him. The feeling changed to that of being trampled by the wild steer's hooves.

My fingers scrabbled a grab of wet sand, and I flung it into his face. Then we rolled over, and we were both in the water.

We came up spluttering, a couple of yards between us and widening into more—*he* was backing off, and leaving me possession of the battlefield.

Then, by the light of the two flashlights, I saw he had a gun. And it was aimed at me!

"Hands—*Svederup!*" he said.

"Pat," I said.

We were both breathing hard, mine hurting my ribs.

"Svederup, what the hell are you doing here?" Pat was out of uniform and in workpants and a sweatshirt.

"What are you?" I asked.

"I thought I heard a scream for help," he said. "I was investigating."

"By means of your sense of smell?"

"Huh?"

"Investigating in the dark."

"Naturally I laid low," he said, "when I saw a suspicious character snooping around with a flashlight. Now, what the hell are you up to?"

"I've been looking into places where somebody might be drinking and feeding a jukebox at 2:30 A.M.," I said, "and one place I looked was Ye Olde Crowe's Neste, if you must know."

"It's 3 A.M., and the place closed an hour ago."

"You sure?"

"Yeah," said Pat. "I was sitting parked up by the pier waiting for one of these boat-owners to show up. When I heard the scream."

"Any particular boat-owner?"

"Pick up your flashlight and let's go," said Pat.

We walked a while silently, his light playing on the sand and mine searching the water.

"I told you I intended to check into that Ensenada proposition," Pat said presently.

"You sure keep busy on your days and nights off."

Patterson answered grumpily, but reasonably. "There's nothing wrong in bucking for plain-clothes, is there?"

We said no more about it. Because at that moment, my flash-beam made the discovery. It was just something whitish and might easily have been mistaken for a hunk of canvas lost off one of the yachts. But then the cop's brighter flashlight came to bear on it, and we saw the glimmer of silver lamé.

We waded out to our chests and carried Dottie Vonn's body ashore.

THIRTEEN

BY TEN O'CLOCK the following morning, I had quite an acquaintance with the San Diego homicide squad team of O'Quill and Lowden.

O'Quill was a thinnish, black-haired, Sphynx-eyed, dry-toned man who chain-smoked Kents. He gave the impression of taciturnity, but he did the talking for both. Lowden, who looked almost affably openfaced, said next to nothing.

They seemed fairly well acquainted with me; only it was a me I didn't know, and would have sneaked up back alleys to avoid meeting socially.

These homicide dicks knew I had an exorbitantly expensive lodging with a close-up view of the Chaparral House pool—was it so I could whet my illicit passions by watching the lady guests in bathing?

The knew I had gone to Ye Olde Crowe's Neste and left with Miss June Betts, the barmaid, a phony business card—and was that how I lured my victims to their doom?

They knew I had lured Dottie Vonn to the Maritime Room and had plied her with liquor in the presence of Steve Gage and Del Bolling.

They knew there had been wild drinking and carousing in Dottie's apartment, and they had Apartment H in to identify me as the guy seen there during the night.

They had the word of a pizza restaurant waitress, a Miss Iole Arkle, that I had been loitering in the neighborhood and had tried to waylay *her* at the bus stop.

They had my fingerprints on the coffee pot; they had a pair of rubber waders in my station wagon; they had the scratches on my face.

They wondered if I had put on the waders and carried a dead-drunk Dottie out into the water and held her head under? They wondered if I had forgotten a clue in the apartment and had gone back to get it and was throwing that into the water when Officer Patterson nailed me?

Naturally, I had some clever retorts to his questions: Why would I have pointed out the body to Patterson if I was the one who put it in the water? Why would I have deliberately woke Apartment H when the door was unlocked? Why wouldn't a man traveling through the Yellowstone and Zion trout stream country have a pair of fishing waders?

Then O'Quill and Lowden left me alone for a time to talk to someone eise in the next room. But soon they came back.

Was it true Del Bolling had given me Dottie Vonn's name as a party girl? and had Del as good as suggested I look her up? and why hadn't I said so in the first place?

I couldn't tell if Del was trying to get me out or in deeper.

They left me alone some more to talk to somebody else in the next room. Again they came back.

Was it true Steve Gage had been the one who plied Dottie with the Maritime Room drinks under the impression she was a prospective tenant for an apartment? and why hadn't I said that in the first place?

Exit again. When they came back, O'Quill asked if I had telephoned Nelda Crossway and Pat Patterson from my hotel around 11 P.M. and if I had been in my room at 2:30 A.M. to take a phone call?

Next, they sprung the mail on me. There were two envelopes

that the cops had picked up at Chaparral House early that morning. A thin blue business envelope and a fat white personal one.

"Legally, you have to open these," said O'Quill, "or we have to get a court order."

I opened the thin blue one first. It bore a *Hook, Line, and Sinker Magazine* return address, and had been forwarded by Florrie Schultz. I expected it to be a chance to renew my subscription at the special bargain rate, but what fell out but a check for fifteen dollars in payment for my manuscript entitled, "Flyfishing for Carp Can Be Fun!"

You have to be a beginning author to appreciate an event like the first sale. I tried to give O'Quill and Lowden the idea, though. I did a few dance steps, shook hands all around, and offered to set up the morning coffee. . . .

"Well, maybe that explains the waders," said O'Quill. "Now what about the other envelope?"

The other was from Florrie Schultz.

Dear Ken, she had written, *I hope the H-L-S letter contains what it seems to contain, but don't let it turn you into a pot-boiling hack. You are capable of so much finer things than catching carp and murderers. Which reminds me, a travel agency out there has been frantically long-distance 'phoning trying to ascertain your whereabouts, and I trust you have not done some prankish elfin thing to offend Mr. Crossway. . . .*

"What does this mean?" said O'Quill.

"What could it mean?" I said. "The notoriously rich and unscrupulous H. H. Crossway wished to bump off an unemployed night club singer, so he imported one of his Minnesota mob for the job."

Lowden made one of his rare interruptions. "You could be much funnier if you had a few hours in a cell to prepare your script."

I told them about the Canadian Jones scoop. "Mr. Crossway provided the expense-paid trip as an award," I said. "Actually, I didn't earn it. I merely have a nose for news that keeps leading me accidentally to where the headlines are happening."

"You haven't explained the insurance-company-card gag, either," said O'Quill.

"Why," I said, "I had the prankish elfin idea of letting it get back to Mr. Crossway that I had signed up for a different job, and he might've raised my wages."

They let me go. Not because they believed anything I said, but because somebody had opened Ye Olde Crowe's Neste, and found the suicide note slipped in under the door.

O'Quill and Lowden didn't show me the note. It was in the next room, I guess.

I walked out through an anteroom, where the Iole Arkle character recoiled from me. Out in a corridor, Steve Gage broke off talking to Petterson to shake my hand. "I imagine they gave you a rough go," he said. "Me, too."

"Why you?"

"Because they need some new blood in the detective division," said Pat. "I told them she had a record of a previous suicide attempt. Well, they know now."

I wondered if O'Quill and Lowden had suspected him for a while.

"Oh, their incredulity was legitimate," Steve said. "They questioned why an unemployed entertainer would wish to move from her inexpensive apartment out to much more costly La Jolla."

"Why would she?"

"I don't know," said Steve, "unless Patterson is right and she wanted the gas oven to put her head into. Anyway, I don't appreciate being aroused at five in the morning and loaded into a squad car to guess at the answer."

"You birds want to squeeze in my truck?" said Patterson.

"I telephoned Ava," said Steve, "and Kelly has my car outside."

"Then I can head for Claremont," said Pat.

"Yes, you ride with me, Ken," said Steve.

The San Diego police department has a parking area right at the headquarters' front door, and we had no trouble picking out a peach-complexion Cadillac among the official black, white-trimmed sedans. Not with Kelly waving from the window of the Caddie.

"I was beginning to think you just used Ava's," I said.

Steve gave me a funny look. In the morning sunlight, he needed a shave. Being darker, I probably showed the need more.

"Somebody dented a fender for me," he said. "It's in the shop about every other week, but if you don't drive a Cadillac you're not a realtor. You are blackballed by the Association. Hop in, Ken."

Kelly slid over and pushed open the door on the other side. I got in, and those Cadillacs are built wide but it was a not unintimate seating arrangement.

"Your bus is around the harbor, isn't it?" Steve said. "Drop you there."

We nosed into traffic.

"I had your radio on, Steve," Kelly said. "Listening like mad. But what really happened?"

She looked very fresh and girlish in a summery, lilac-colored, puffy-sleeved affair. Her interest could have passed for normal girlish curiosity, but of course I remembered mentioning Dottie Vonn's name at the quaint drive-in.

"A routine suicide investigation," Steve said. "The worst was the officers waking Brad to see me marched off. There might be serious consequences, psychologically—that's the part I'm sorry about."

It had been a long gravelly night for me and for numerous other people besides a kid who undoubtedly witnessed more harrowing scenes on TV every day of his life, and a block or so down Pacific Highway, I said, "The person I feel sorriest for is Dottie Vonn."

"It's tragic for anyone to take one's own life," Kelly said. "She couldn't have had any connection with Bob, could she?"

The power brakes snapped us up at the Broadway intersection red light. If he made many stops like that, I could see where the fender repair bills could mount up. And on the rebound, Kelly landed practically in my lap.

"We wouldn't necessarily know about that," Steve said. "A cop in there was telling me Miss Vonn made an earlier attempt on her life in La Jolla some years ago. She apparently received transfusions from Bob and seems afterward to have neglected or refused to pay him."

The light changed. Steve resumed driving.

"Is that *official?*" asked Kelly, who had slid off my lap but, from the sound of her voice, had had the breath knocked out of her.

"It was this one cop's story."

"Patterson," I said.

"How would *he* know?" said Kelly.

Patterson intrigued *me*, too.

"I can't imagine," Steve Gage said. He gunned the Caddie over into the left-hand lane; luckily the driver right behind in that lane had power brakes also.

"It doesn't seem likely Miss Vonn would have boasted of such dead-beat tactics," Steve said. "Bob wouldn't have told anybody. He wouldn't have dunned or sued her. Money meant nothing to him."

"I disagree, Steve," said Kelly in a firm young voice. "Money meant as much to Bob as to anyone else."

The Cadillac was swinging from the left lane over onto Harbor Drive.

"Bob was raised in luxury," Kelly went on, "but being thrown on his own taught him the value of a dollar."

I could understand how it might.

"Furthermore," said Kelly, "Bob resented frauds and sharp-shooters. He had the lowest possible opinion of cheats and swindlers and dollar-grabbing phonies."

A half-grin wrinkled the side of Steve's Indian-tanned face visible to me. "Nelda," he said. "Bob resented Nelda for those and other reasons. But I question whether he lay awake nights brooding about money matters."

"Bob *cared* about money, and that's what made his life so wonderful," Kelly said. "In spite of it, he cared still more for self-respect and integrity. The terrific thing about Bob was that, liking wealth as much as the next man, he had the spunk to shrug off his father's fortune."

She stared straight ahead, and I couldn't decide whether she was explaining Bob to Steve or to me or even to herself. Anyway, it was clear how Ava got the idea Bob Crossway had been Kelly's first and maybe only love.

The same idea might have penetrated Steve's thinking, for he said, much more gently, "Bob was a sweet guy. Most people change, but to the end he remained a genuine idealist. Not mercenary at all."

Kelly became almost angry. "He wasn't any angel, either," she said sharply. "He knew what he wanted of life, and he was tough enough to fight for and get it."

Right then, and for the first time, I began to see how a man would be lucky to have her on his team—somebody, for example, in a fellow's corner during the tough rounds with the O'Quills and Lowdens. That pair had actually sized me up for a sex-fiend killer, and I still felt kind of dirtied from watching the reflection of myself in their crime-calloused eyes.

Steve was silent, steering us on past the Naval Station, but then he came out with something that made me wonder whether Ava had been coaching him: "A lot of us don't sell our souls for filthy lucre. I'm sure Ken here wouldn't."

"I never had the chance," I said.

"Exactly," said Kelly. "The temptation faced Bob every day he lived. He could have become incredibly rich by merely playing the phony until his father passed on."

Steve gave it thought. "True," he said, "but it is also true that Bob always had an out. He had a reserve of security that Ken and I and you yourself don't have. If he really urgently needed money, got in a jam where he *had* to have ready cash, he knew where he could raise any amount of it. Very few of us know the feeling of being able to lay ten thousand dollars on the line if the situation should arise."

What situation? All I could think of was that remark of Dottie's about taking ten grand from Bob.

"You're in the wrong lane," said Kelly.

"Oh," said Steve.

He stuck out his arm and made the turn anyway. We slid around the ship chandler's corner and into the parking area. My station wagon was there, all right, and Del Bolling's *Adventure II* was out on the water.

"I don't take anything away from Bob, either," said Steve softly. "Only we don't necessarily know the whole inside story of his or any other person's life. It is well to keep the fact in mind, and avoid some cruel disillusionments. Besides, we have to go on living our own lives."

He had something there.

"Ken," he said, "why don't you take Miss Kelly in your car; I have to stop at the Pacific Beach Trust and Security on an escrow matter."

FOURTEEN

RETURNING TO La Jolla, Kelly and I didn't find much to say; boy and girl don't when thrown together with words of advice that could easily be set to wedding march music.

Besides, I was brooding hard over two items. First, Steve Gage knew more than he would tell—at least tell in front of Kelly. And then Patterson kept me intrigued. If he was really bucking for plainclothes, why hadn't he told the dicks a lot more than their questions indicated they knew?

I dropped Kelly at the travel agency. At Chaparral House I showered and shaved and got the valet service to promise to return the imported Italian pure silk before the 5 P.M checking-out hour. With the grandchild dead, why would H. H. Crossway keep me longer on the assignment?

I drove on up the hill and found the newspaper magnate troweling fertilizer around the roots of his pet roses. I gave him the fill-in while he chewed a cold cigar which he said the doctors forbade him to light before lunch.

"The story has the ring of truth," the President and Founder decided.

"Which story? Dottie Vonn told several stories."

"The ten thousand dollar part," the old man said. "Giving some unknown and uninvestigated woman such a sum of money is exactly and characteristically what Robert would have done."

"Yuh, Steve Gage says money meant nothing to him. But Miss Kelly claims the opposite. How do you vote?"

"It wasn't the money primarily," Crossway said, "it was his independence. He couldn't come to me, his father, for advice. Oh no, and he couldn't let my attorneys handle it."

The money still looked fairly primary to me. "Steve Gage once mentioned your son put a second mortgage on the Casa Luna Vista," I said. "Could your attorneys find out if that's a ten thousand dollar mortgage?"

"Certainly; any lien would have to be on record. But I don't doubt the story, and that part is more or less routine and immmaterial."

"It's material why she first said Bob gave her a couple of hundred down and a few hundred more from time to time and later changed to a flat ten grand," I said. "What was running through her head?"

Mr. Crossway threw at me an elderly clubman's worldly wise look. "Women of that stripe have only two things in their heads. Sex and money, and the sex is a means to money."

"Specifically?"

"She had realized ten thousand dollars from that child. She obviously wished to minimize the amount, for fear of being prosecuted for blackmail and extortion."

I gave it a half-nod.

"Later on she thought, or somebody pointed out to her, that the ten thousand settlement constituted the strongest proof that Bob *was* the father."

"Who?" I said.

"Women of that stripe always are the tools of sex racketeers," the clubman said. "The man, whoever he was, saw the prospect of further and immensely larger profits from my grandchild."

"But the child is dead."

"That *can't* be. No matter who or what the mother was, the child is Robert's and my last living descendant. The child *must* and *can* be found. . . ."

And here among the rose bushes stood no intelligently astute clubman and board chairman but a tired old duffer with a chewed-up cigar drooping from his mouth, with one lingering, frantic hope in those faded blue eyes.

Sentimental feelings stirred me, looking at him. But *he* tried to deny his own sentimentality. "I'm a realist, Svederup, and a hardheaded one. And I say to you that Dottie Vonn would never have let this potentially valuable child slip through her fingers."

Still, the kid could have been run over in the street accidentally. Or, as I had thought in the Maritime Room, she might have said the child was dead in the hope of herself collecting the insurance. In that case, I had goofed, played the thing all wrong, struck out with the winning run on base. I should have bunted—instead of going in there like a rookie slugging for a homer against big-time pitching.

"Well, Dottie's dead and can't tell us different now," I said. But I didn't believe Dottie died by suicide any more than I believed Bob Crossway died by accident.

"The man behind Dottie wouldn't let the child slip through his fingers, either," said the President and Founder.

Somebody out there was throwing a mighty mean curve—that much I believed. But we all have our beliefs, and H. H. Crossway stood firmly on his: "Somebody besides the Vonn girl *must* know and *must* be traced . . ."

I studied the owner of thirty-eight newspapers worth five million dollars who couldn't indulge in a forenoon cigar and might not live five more years; I thought of who would get the dough when he died; but mostly I mused that Bob was one, Dottie made two, and they say sudden death occurs by threes. The kid, if alive, could be the third.

It seemed the Milquevais rookie might do better at the bat if he had someone helping by stealing the other side's signals. "Mr. Crossway," I said, "would you be willing to raise your sights? Could you think in bigger terms than my present salary and this hotel room at half-price press rates?"

The chairman of the board, again, regarded me.

"Have you some of Robert in you?" I asked. "Would you lay the cash on the line, a big hunk of it and in cash? And no running to your attorneys, no releases or receipts or guarantees of any kind?"

He continued staring at me and I felt as though I were some filthy aphid or mealy bug that had infested his Billy Graham rose.

He went for it, though.

"How much do you want, Svederup?" And it showed how hardheaded a realist he was where this grandchild figured.

"A hundred a week," I said. "And as far as that goes, I know where I can get a cheaper roof over my head."

"But . . ."

"Mr. Crossway, I happen to have met an individual. I don't say he can be greased, but still he would probably appreciate having the first trust mortgage paid off on *his* home. Some little favor like that."

FIFTEEN

HE WAS a perfectly small *d* democratic millionaire, willing to ride down to the village in a second-hand station wagon and be seen on the streets in his gardening garb.

The branch Bank of America cheerfully accepted the H. H. Crossway countercheck and handed him a thousand dollars. Ten C-notes really made no more of a wad than so many singles, but still they gave the concept of how ten grand would have bulged Dottie's stocking. If she had banked it, there must have been microfilm records of the transaction. Five hundred miles and a couple of days just to find out?

"Shouldn't we mark this money?" the old man said.

"You better keep your money here in the bank, if it's the money you care about."

"As a sensible business precaution, at least copy the serial numbers."

"Suppose he looks at me with lie detector eyes and I flunk the test."

"Oh."

"If you're going to fish, Mr. Crossway, you must risk bait."

And if I was going to fish for him, I had to know he could put up a lot more than $1000 without quibbling.

He took a cab home. I stepped back inside the bank and copied off the serial numbers and found a bank officer to verify and initial and file away the list.

Then I headed for Steve Gage's office. "Out to lunch," the sign said. I walked back to use the phone at the Rexall drugstore and listened to the robot request my message.

"Dear Steve," I said, "I'm taking Bob's apartment. Yours truly, Ken."

Next I phoned Pat Patterson. "Can't you let a guy get some sleep?" he said. "Oh, well, come on over."

With the help of a Rexall-purchased street guide, I found the cop's address. It was across Highway 101 and the Santa Fe tracks, a ranch house with an open garage door revealing the camp-trailer truck inside and Pat's patched wet suit hanging up to dry on the side wall with some masks and a couple of arbalete guns.

Pat wasn't sleeping; he was with the family in the back yard, and it gave me a shock: I hadn't thought of Patterson as a family man. But there he was, wearing old, faded, lifeguard-red swim trunks, working at setting up a slightly larger-than-bath-tub-sized plastic wading pool.

His wife stood by, holding the garden hose, ready to fill the plastic ring. She was a pony-tailed, shy-faced woman who flung me one glance and thereafter kept her lids downcast.

Their kid was about Brad Gage's size but looked younger and not so bright owing to the thumb-in-the-mouth habit. The kid reminded me of somebody—the jumpy Iole Arkle character, possibly. He was a nervous thumb-sucker, and he could have sensed a tension among the grownups.

"Hello, Pat," I said.

He grunted something too short to be misconstrued as an introduction to his wife and offspring.

"My, my," I said, "wouldn't it be dandy if you had a regulation pool here?"

Another grunt.

"You got the room for it. Level enough too."

"You aware what those deals cost?" he said, irritated.

"Two, three thousand?"

"Three, four thousand. By the time you pay for the filtration system and the tiling and the fence. The new ordinance says you have to fence out the neighborhood kids, and a cop has to follow the law."

He seemed to half-expect an argument over the last statement. "In other words," I said, "you have the room, and you'd like a pool, and it's just a question of the financing."

"You catch on quick."

"Oh, I was thinking of it when I called you up," I said.

He caught on quick. He looked at me, then he looked at his wife:

"Liz, why don't you and Sonny go look at some TV?"

He had Liz well trained. The kid, too—except that the thumb-sucking habit was going to lead to a fancy tooth-wiring job.

Pat waited for the back door to close. "Where do you get your ideas, anyway?" he said then.

"Crowd I run around with. Capitalists who could buy you a pool and never miss it."

"Who?"

"I didn't mention *your* name to him."

"Oh."

"So I shan't mention *his* name to you." I fancied Officer Patterson could guess the mystery sponsor. He knew I was an employee of the President and Founder.

"What's your capitalist want?" His face remained Stone Aged.

"The low-down on Dottie Vonn." I opened three fingers one after the other. "Did she ever bear a child? Who was the father? Where is that child now?"

No change altered the cop's paleolithic expression. He appeared as dumb as a college athlete being quizzed on the subject of subsidized football. What *was* a football?—that kind of dumbness.

"Girl who drowned last night," I prompted.

"Why ask me about her?"

"Different reasons. One is you're a cop, and you know how to find out things."

He seemed satisfied with reason number one. Some rival college subsidized its players? He could discuss that.

"Oh, the proposition is for me to do private investigating during my off-duty time?"

"You're doing that anyway, aren't you?"

I knew the danger of needling Pat. He might pull the badge act and arrest me for attempting to bribe an officer. But his thick hide scarcely felt the needle.

"Oh, sure," said Pat, "if I hear a scream for help, I investigate."

There had been no scream. At least, none that nervous Iole Arkle overheard. She would not have remained alone at a bus stop in a lonely dark fog that contained a scream for help. Not if she had to kick through the pizza place's glass front door.

"A second reason," I said, "is that you trade favors with Del Bolling. He might whisper you the answers."

This amused Officer Patterson. He grinned his derision. "Your capitalist wouldn't give a spit, say nothing of a pool, for anything Del swore on a stack of Bibles."

"I'm not buying Bibles. Official records and affidavits."

Pat stopped grinning.

"Wait a minute," he said. "I thought you wanted, uh, verbal confidential information. You expect all this in black and white, signed, sealed and delivered?"

"You don't want just the blueprint of a pool, do you? Something concrete you can *use*."

The cop shook his head.

"Not enough to risk my tail out in the open. I don't want it."

It was a stubborn case, requiring the needle all the way in to the hilt, so I went on pushing: "What were you risking last night when you tracked the sand into Dottie's apartment?"

Patterson's exlifeguard's legs dropped him into a crouch; he appeared ready to take me out with one punch.

He hesitated, however. Seemed to debate whether to kill me or laugh it off. If he killed me, where would he hide this body? The plastic pool wasn't any Pacific Ocean or San Diego Harbor.

But of course I could not read his thoughts, only my own. He said, "You're kidding." He wasn't wholly in the sway of Neanderthal passions, after all.

"No," I said, "I think seriously you were going to meet Del at the Neste. He hadn't showed up by closing time, and after hanging around outside for nearly another hour, you decided to interview Dottie instead. You hiked up the beach to Dulcine Street and found the door unlocked, nobody at home."

He straightened from the ready-crouch. I meant his college, but some other player on the team. He could still discuss it.

"What would I want of Dottie?" he said.

"Sex or money." I quoted from the clubman's book.

"I'm not hard enough up for the first to be stood up until 3 A.M.," said Pat. "And the second she didn't have."

"You knew her, then?"

He seemed to resume debating my fate.

"I don't care," I said. "If you're already in action and warmed up to go, so much the better. I only want to know *was* there a child, and *whose*, and *where*. Three little words that could put you and yours into a regulation-sized, filtrated, and fenced swimming pool."

"You say."

"This says." I opened my wallet and separated Mr. Crossway's thousand from the fifteen-dollar *Hook, Line, and Sinker* check.

Pat did not hold out his hand for the money; but neither did he clench his fist and knock me down for the insult. "I'd need a few hours to sleep on this," he said. "I need a few hours' sleep, period."

I put the ten C-notes down on the little plastic pool's rim.
"You can return these if the answer is no," I said. "You'll find me in Bob's old apartment."

Sure, he could return the money. Several times on the return trip to Chaparral House I reminded myself that I was not forcing an honest cop to betray his professional code of ethics. He knew where to find the homicide squad office if he preferred the upright life.

Back at Chaparral House, I again tried to phone Steve. The robot answered.

I packed the suitcase, and tried to catch up some sleep myself, but there seemed to be a kind of mosquito invisibly humming around. At a quarter of five, valet service returned the suit. I conquered superstition and put it on.

The robot still answered for Steve.

I turned in the key and gave the boy another two bucks for carrying the suitcase to the wagon. He was an older boy than myself, and probably used his tips to support a family. Men do support families, and without grifting.

Then I drove by Steve's office, but he wasn't there. He was in another escrow deal, or was having another fender mended. Or he had just got off his tail and had gone out after business.

I didn't like the prospect of moving into Bob's apartment without definitely knowing Steve had played back the robot message cylinder. But I had another errand in mind, anyway.

SIXTEEN

THE WALRUS-MUSTACHED barman had no leisure for TV viewing. He was holding spellbound a half-dozen Ye Olde Crowe's Neste customers. They looked as though they might be regulars, and if so, they would have seen or heard Dottie Vonn around. So I got into the huddle and bowed my head over a beer glass to avoid the barmaid's glance. It was not necessary to ask many questions.

Walrus-Mustache had been the one who unlocked the door and found the suicide note, and he was telling about it: "It said she had lost the only man she could ever have loved, and had lost her baby, and none of us would ever see her any more."

The note seemed to have made no direct mention of an intention to drown herself.

"But how often I watched her by the window here," the barman continued. "She'd be gazing toward the pier and looking like she might one day leap off it."

He knew why. "Dottie's trouble wasn't drink," he said, "it was whatever drove her to drink. It always is."

The notion that Dottie Vonn's death might have been anything other than suicide clearly had not entered his head. Self-destruction accorded perfectly with every observation he had ever made of her temperament.

"I had a feeling that doom was overhanging her when she first walked in here two weeks ago."

I signaled for a second beer, then interrupted the monologue. "Has Del Bolling been in today?" I said.

"No, sir," the barman said. "Ed was, a while ago."

"Was Del in last night?" I said.

"Late," the barman said. "Around closing time."

It sounded as if Pat Patterson had stood up Del.

"I had a feeling of the same doom," the barman was saying, "the minute I saw that piece of paper on the floor."

I walked out, and kept my face turned from the pizza windows in order not to frighten Iole Arkle. Out in the yacht corral a small boat was bobbling up and down beside the larger *Adventurer II*. I waved from the pier.

Ed was on deck, and peered toward me. He turned his head, and Del Bolling appeared from the galley or someplace and peered at me through the dark sunglasses. He nodded, and Ed got into the dinghy, and rowed over to take me out to the vabin cruiser.

"I've been thinking about you," Del Bolling greeted me.

The yachtsman apparently wore his yachting clothes only when ashore. He had on a white silk neck scarf, a jacket that an Englishman might have taken to a cricket match, and beautiful pearl doeskin-fabric slacks.

"In fact, I phoned Chaparral House several times, and the last time they said you had checked out."

Come to think of it, I was as hard to find as Steve.

"I've been thinking of you, too, Del," I said. "I understand you went to bat for me with the dicks, is that right?" I could see nothing in the big butterfly sunglasses except twin reflections of myself.

"I wanted to save you for that trip to Ensenada."

"No. Seriously?"

"Seriously. I realized I had alluded to Dottie in somewhat playful terms. I assumed you, being a long way from home, felt playful and managed to date her." He smiled nicely. "If that's what you want, I know of some high-spirited senoritas in Ensenada who won't land us in jail."

"Some other time," I said. "Did you check up last night to see if I took Dottie safely home?"

"Yes," said Del. "Yes, I did. How did you know?"

"You seemed so solicitous of her."

"I was," he said. "I tried to phone her apartment before leaving the Maritime Room. The line was busy, though. Well, it might have been a two-party line or even a four-party line. It could have been one of the other parties, and on my way down here I stopped at the apartment. She was still gabbing on the phone then."

"When?" I said.

"Elevenish," said Del.

"Gabbing with who?"

A tiny pained frown came and went from the brow above the sunglasses.

"Gabbing with *whom?*" I said.

He smiled. "The cop."

"Patterson?"

"Yes," said Del. "This is off the record. At headquarters I tried to spare both you and Pat. No sense involving you two because a depressive girl went over the verge."

"What was she gabbing to Pat *about?*" I asked.

The skipper thought briefly. "They had mutual acquaintances to talk about," he said. "You would have to know all about Dottie. I'm getting under way here in a few minutes, and I lack the time to tell you her life story."

"Do you know her life story?"

"Who knows anyone's life story? I tried to help the girl get onto her feet. She told me things. I help a lot of people—become interested in a lot of people."

"Maybe you should tell me *your* life story," I said.

His lips smiled. "*That* would certainly be too long a tale."

"Look, Del. If I went along with you to Ensenada, would you tell me about Dottie?"

The rest of his face joined in the smile. "I've been trying to suggest it all along."

But I shook my head. There was the Patterson thing. There was the obvious fact that both Del and Nelda wanted me out of the way. "I can't spare the time," I said.

"Edward," said the skipper.

Ed strode up and bulged his tattoo-overlaid muscles into an eyebrow touching salute.

"Our guest wishes to go ashore," Del said. "I failed to twist his arm hard enough."

The salute changed to a crashing fist. It must have been his fist. The cabin cruiser couldn't have capsized, as it seemed.

I flew backward, caught at and missed the rail, and landed headfirst in the dinghy. The dinghy capsized. I remember that much, vaguely.

SEVENTEEN

I WOKE UP at sea, much more seasick than the wave-cutting motion of the *Adventure ll* could explain. I recognized the *Adventure ll* from the deck awnings overhead.

The sun hurt my eyes. It was now well down toward the horizon, glaring in under the awning. I sat up and looked the other way and uncertainly made out the thin pencil line of distant land. I could have swum one-tenth that far, given a month in which to train for the ordeal—and if I didn't ache all over, my head especially, and wasn't weighed down by a salt-water-soaked imported Italian pure silk that seemed at least a ton.

"Have a drink?" Del's voice asked.

He occupied the built-in observation chair at the stern and swiveled my way, negligently holding a long, tall glass in his hand.

"Perhaps some coffee from the galley?"

I twisted the other way. I could twist freely. I wasn't bound or gagged—why would I be? Ed up ahead at the cockpit wheel undoubtedly had a spanner or maybe a six-shooter within handy reach. I couldn't take on two men at the opposite ends of a forty-foot boat simultaneously, and I had nowhere to escape except overboard and straight down.

"A change into dry things?" Del said.

I looked at him again, and thought carefully of what to say. It seemed important to make the right opening here. The cynical, self-assured note appeared the best to strike.

"Oh, an Ivy League snatch," I said after long consideration.

He put down the glass. There was a hole bored into the chair arm for him to put it in.

"I'm as much Big Ten as you are," Del said. "How long were you at Iowa, anyway?"

"Semester," I said.

"I took the full four-year law course at Wisconsin," Del said. "The war came along, and the legal training helped me to dabble in surplusage contracts afterward. Legally, your unsupported testimony could not make a kidnapping charge stick. You were invited to make this trip in the presence of a disinterested witness. You discussed the advisability of accepting the invitation with another witness. You checked out of your hotel under your own power, and you came aboard of your own free will. You could have so easily just fallen overboard in a landlubberly attempt to help cast off and get under way."

He was so nearly right.

Of course, I had told Steve's robot I meant to take Bob's apartment. And I had told Pat Patterson he could find me there. Only what if Pat just kept the ten C-notes and said nothing?

Here I was miles from dry land and heeling southward at fifteen to twenty knots, a helpless prisoner on the deep in which Bob Crossway and Dottie Vonn had already perished. What if *Adventure II* arrived at Ensenada minus a passenger?

"Maybe I will stagger to the galley after some coffee," I said. Possibly I could set fire to the galley, or get into the head and open a sea cock, and thus force my kidnappers to run their craft aground.

"You needn't stagger anywhere," said Del. "Oh, Liz, the coffee."

And here appeared Liz Patterson with the steaming cup. She wore the same pony-tail as before, wore the same housedress, and had added no make-up to her face. She had taken off her shoes, probably because bare feet cling better to a deck.

She gave me the one look, and with downcast eyes handed me the cup.

"What's all this about?" I said.

"It's another long story," said Del Bolling. "You'd better hear it from Liz's own lips."

He picked up his glass and went forward, or bowward—up to the front end of the boat. Liz sat down in the observation chair. Her bare toes wriggled on the deck planking. I sipped at the importer's specially blended coffee; Liz brewed it better than Ed did.

She looked so much like any ordinary young housewife, good at making coffee and embarrassed by a strange man gazing at her bare feet.

"Well," she finally said, "I overheard that proposition you put up to Pat."

I now recalled there'd been no loud TV noises from the house while Pat and I dickered.

"I don't know why he didn't clobber you," Liz said. "He would have, before they put him on that La Jolla beat. He's worked on too many riot calls to champagne parties and burglaries where the woman left her $30,000 pearls in the bureau drawer. He gets to thinking of what they have and don't need, and we don't have and could use."

It rubs off on you, as Steve and Kelly both said.

"We had so much hard luck right from the start," Liz said. "Losing the first and not able to have any of our own."

Right then I saw through it, and who wouldn't have? I should have realized at once who Sonny Patterson reminded me of. The toddler in the snapshot. The hand pushing the thumb into his mouth had covered up the characteristic chin. . . .

These housewives don't spend all their time making coffee. They put in some of it crying, and they go on their knees to pray. I recognized tears and prayer in Liz's voice. In a sudden attack of near hysteria, she panicked into beating her fist on the chair arm.

"They can't take my baby away from me. . . ." She sobbed.

So I felt like a rat, although rats don't feel that way about it.

"What makes you think they can, if you legally adopted him?" I said.

The tears made her look less like a young housewife, more like a frightened girl having a homesick first day at a new school.

"I saw a piece in the newspaper not so long ago. A couple adopted a child from the natural mother, and years later the natural father got the adoption annulled because he never signed *his* consent . . ."

She even had the newspaper clip with her, but I had too much of a headache to bother reading it.

"You didn't get Sonny from an agency, then?" I said.

"The agencies don't like when you're of different faiths as Pat and I are." I remembered the medal on his chest when he went skin diving. All the little pieces might be moving here into a pattern.

"And," Liz went on, "Pat heard of a girl, a show girl in Las Vegas, who wanted to put her child out in a foster home."

"Who'd he hear *from?*"

"I don't know. Some friend. It could have been some other cop. Anybody. Pat doesn't tell me about his friends."

Not that much of a family man.

"And Pat went up there and brought Sonny home with him," said Liz.

"*You* didn't go along?"

"No," said Liz.

There was a reason for that, and she admitted it.

"I didn't even know if he went to Las Vegas," she said. "Pat might have been the father, himself, for all I knew. He'd been a lifeguard that summer before Sonny was born, and a lifeguard meets some—you know—willing girls."

Her bare toes wriggled on the decking.

"Anyway, I just fell in love with Sonny. I nursed him through the measles and mumps and whooping cough. You wouldn't *know.* I kept after Pat, and finally we both went to Las Vegas and talked to the girl and she agreed to the adoption. She was a brown-eyed blonde, and Pat has dark eyes, so he wasn't the father after all. It had to be a blue-eyed man."

Bob Crossway had been blue-eyed. And Steve Gage still was. And Del Bolling was at least pale-eyed—the one time I ever saw him come out from behind the black butterfly panes.

"What was Sonny's name on the adoption paper?" I said.

"It was kind of awful," said Liz. "Jackpots Vonn Smith."

So that tied into Dottie Vonn's statements. It all tied in with her talk and her suicide note. The note said she had lost the only man she could ever have loved, and Bob Crossway was certainly lost for keeps. And if she had let the kid be adopted, she had lost him, too.

I imagined it would all interest H. H. Crossway intensely.

"Mrs. Patterson," I said, "look at it like this. Suppose you and Pat got a nice settlement, really fixed you up financially, and you knew Sonny would have a fine home and the best education and be *rich* some day . . ."

"No," she said. "He's mine. I won't give up my baby for all the money there *is*."

She meant it.

"You're excited. Maybe after you think it over a few days—?"

"I've thought it over for days. Sonny needs *love*. He doesn't *say* much, but Sonny is sensitive, and he doesn't miss a thing. He feels all the squabbling in the air, and already it's put him back to sucking his thumb."

The sun had gone down while we talked. The sea and the sky had grown darker.

"Squabbling?"

"Pat talking like you're talking," Liz said.

The dark air felt chillier.

"What started Pat talking like this?" I said.

"He doesn't tell me a damn thing. It's got so I don't believe him, anyway. I've been running around myself like crazy, trying to find the natural father and get him to sign the adoption papers."

The coffee had cooled to lukewarm.

"I suppose you asked Dottie Vonn," I said.

"I couldn't find *her*. Not in time."

The water-soaked imported Italian pure silk kept out none of the cold air.

"Who else?"

"Del Bolling," said Liz. "Here last Christmas he gave Sonny a fifty-dollar sidewalk bike. He couldn't help me, but he sure was nice. . . ."

"Who else?"

"Nobody that knew anything. Then you came along today. Pat works the four-to-twelve shift, so as soon as he left the house I hired a baby-sitter and rushed to see Del. Because he was so nice before."

But not nice enough to have linked Dottie Vonn's name with Bob Crossway.

Del walked over to us. "You're shivering, Liz. Slip into something warm."

She barefooted away, well trained.

Del sat down in the observation chair. He observed me. He had removed the big dark glasses. His eyes were steely in the waning light.

"I'm an orphan myself," said Del. "Nobody ever gave me any

fifty-dollar bikes at Christmas. So I gave the cop's kid one, and
I suppose gave it to myself vicariously."

"Good legal point," I said.

He observed me steadily. "Legally, a living natural father could
easily have won custody. A grandparent can't, particularly a
grandparent neither of whose two sons ever acknowledged this
child. On the other hand, an ungodly rich grandparent could possibly persuade one of the adoptive parents to say the adoption
had been a black market baby transaction. It might then be annulled under the constitutional amendment which prohibits the
sale of human beings as chattel slaves."

I fancied H. H. Crossway's attorneys would explore this and all
other possible legal steps.

"Not the kind of business I would care to dabble in myself,"
said Del. He seemed honest at this minute. "How about you?"

So I stopped worrying about his honesty, and Patterson's ethics,
and instead took a look at Kenneth Svederup.

How about this Courthouse Kid?

I faced a choice here.

"If Liz's story is true," I said, "I wouldn't touch that business
with an eleven-foot pole."

"Then I don't think we would get any farther by continuing on
to Ensenada," said the mild-voiced skipper. "Oh, Ed. Turn back."

It all seemed so smooth and friendly and *right* at the time.

EIGHTEEN

Adventure II slid in under the headland's old Spanish lighthouse
and throbbed up the San Diego harbor channel. Downtown lights
thrust long streaky lances rushing to meet us. The channel was
loomed over by the burly shapes of USN flattops and tenders,
vibrated over by music from Shelter Island. A masthead toward
North Island chewed and spat out green splinters of code. A lot
of corn-belt kids join the Navy to see this much of the world.

Personally, I would have liked to be somewhere else and a long
distance from it all. What *if* Sonny was Bob and Dottie's kid, better off without the Crossway money while he had Liz's loving
care?

And I still had a loud headache, large bruises, and grave misgiv-
ings concerning Pat Patterson. Where had *he* heard of Dottie's
child needing a foster home? Bob Crossway was the only source
I could think of, and Dottie had spoken of Bob's paying for the
child's support. Foster parents get paid . . .

Adventure II berthed among the other yachts and cruisers
around the pier.

"Thanks, Del," said Liz warmly, "you've been really swell."

"Why, I never had a mother myself," said Del, "and I know what having you means to Sonny."

What about this guy? As far as I could see, he hoped to marry Nelda and live high off her hog. It'd be a fatter hog if H. H. Crossway never found his living grandchild. Still, Del was the first to mention Dottie to me.

Ed put us ashore. I took Liz to the station wagon and drove her to the Claremont address and parked in the driveway facing the open, empty garage.

"I only hope the baby-sitter got Sonny to bed all right," Liz said. "You'll just have to tell Pat it was all a mistake. And thanks, you've been swell, too."

I could tell Pat it was all a mistake, and he could still ruin it all on his own.

I drove to La Jolla and the Casa Luna Vista. There was no note from Pat in the letterbox, and no message slipped under the door.

I stripped off the imported Italian jinx. Everything in the pockets came out a sodden mess—traveler's checks, paper money, snapshot, bright virginal *Hook, Line, and Sinker* trophy. The salt water had left me some silver change, though, as life does generally leave a person a little something.

Of course the traveler's checks would be replaced, and probably the magazine editor would forward a duplicate check—though it wouldn't have the same sentimental value.

I swallowed three aspirins from Bob's medicine chest and hot-showered and dressed. Then I drove up the hill to the Crossway chateau.

A Cadillac stood parked before the entrance. Not Steve's. A very solemn, sedate, dark blue Cadillac of the Fleetwood series.

Nelda herself opened the chateau portal. Her smile was cordiality itself, utterly unalloyed with surprise.

"Father Crossway is closeted with his attorney," she said, "and you'll have to wait your turn."

"Fine. Let's me and you get into a closet someplace."

"Let's have a drink first." She led me into a large and sumptuous living room in one corner of which stood a wheeled bar laid out with bottles, decanters, and glasses.

"Sherry, Scotch, bourbon . . ."

From the looks of the glasses, the attorney ahead of me had selected sherry.

"Beer," I said.

"I'll ring for one, and do you mind if I mix myself a wee droppie?"

She bent over the portable bar and the front of her dress gaped slightly open. Well, I supposed a girl who had won a body beautiful contest as far back as '48 must feel a necessity to show she still had what it took then . . .

"You aren't afraid any more," I said.

"I never was. I only sincerely felt it my duty to find out whether Robert had made a will. I know now that he did."

"Yuh?"

"This afternoon the county estate-tax assessor opened Robert's bank box. Robert's will was in there. It left everything to his college buddy, Peter Kelly."

Nelda could not have looked more pleased if the will had conveyed everything to *her*. Could it be she figured it pointed suspicion away from her? Or maybe Del Bolling had been on the phone, telling her I had been fixed and had promised to keep my mouth shut.

"You misjudged me," said she, pouting.

"I didn't misjudge you," I said. "I knew a rich widow just like you back in Milquevais, owned three farms . . ."

"Mmmm. *Rich.*"

"So she married a kind of poolhall loafer, a real smooth snooker shark."

"What's snooker?"

"She got snookered. Run over by a tractor rushing in the alfalfa ahead of a thunder shower."

"It seldom thunders here," said Nelda.

"Her husband was driving the tractor at the time," I said. "*He* wound up with the three farms, which he sold. He used the money to buy the poolhall."

"You honestly are primed with rural folklore," said Nelda. "May I ask, what's the moral?"

"It's never take on a snooker expert. They know all the angles, english, and combinations. Let one talk himself into the game, and it becomes a game of freeze-out. He picks up the chips and gives you the cold shoulder."

A plain-faced, white-capped maid toted in the beer on a tray. It was an imported-from-Holland beer.

"Thanks for the friendly warning," said Nelda, her odalisque eyes laughing at me. "I shall beware of poolhall sharks driving tractors."

"Some of them drive cabin cruisers," I said.

"You don't *drive* cabin cruisers," cried Nelda gaily.

Was this a new and more subtle act of hers?

"Don't be lulled by friendly appearances. He may be another Archimedes, lying in a warm bath and dreaming up the principle of the lever—scheming to put the leverage on *you*."

"It was specific gravity Archimedes discovered in his tub," said Nelda.

You can fence only so long on a diet of three aspirins; you tire of shadowboxing and want to slug. I slugged: "What the hell is the use of hushing everybody else up when Del Bolling can spring the truth on you any time he likes?"

Nelda stared in open-mouthed surprise. Open-mouthed surprise was not an expression she had practiced before a mirror. Still with her mouth open, she began to laugh. It was not a seductive, not a brazenly sirenish laugh—more of a coughing *he-heh-heh*.

Here, I felt, at last was the real Nelda. . . .

"That's rich," she said. "That's a hot one. I wish to Christ Del or anybody else would spring it. Save me putting out money if they did."

That's how she must have talked in the pre-1948 era, before fame and Junior claimed her—nasally, and with a gum-chewer's snap.

"Who are you putting out money to?" I asked. "Patterson?"

The mask returned to Nelda's features. Patterson's name may have had the effect, but it was more probably the Crossway attorney entering the room. He was a silver-maned, *pince-nezed* free-loader looking for a sherry. Nelda graciously poured it.

"You've been a doll," she said to me. "But now why don't you dash along with your disclosures to the study?" She seemed perfectly unconcerned over what I might tell Father Crossway.

I told him nothing. He told me.

"I was right," the President and Founder said. "Robert *did* borrow ten thousand in September, 1953, with a second trust deed as security. Steve Gage had power of attorney and handled it. *You* could have found out by merely asking him."

If I could have caught up with him.

"But continue on," said H. H. Crossway.

I continued on back down the hill and stopped in the village for a hamburger "with"—who cared about onion on my breath now? And three cups of coffee, a very ordinary blend. I traded some silver for more aspirin and a bottle of liniment at the Rexall, then returned to Bob's apartment to await Pat Patterson.

Would he return the money, or sell Sonny to the high bidder? I might have to wait until midnight to find out. The liniment fumes drugged me into dozing on the comfortable sofa in Bob's apartment. It had been a long hard day since 2:30 A.M. . . .

Ten winks later, somebody woke me by scratching a key into the apartment door. Besides myself only Nelda and Steve Gage had keys—that I knew of.

"Come in," I called. Whoever it was, would anyway.

The door opened and Kelly stepped inside.

"Ken!"

"Kelly."

Then both together: "What are you doing here?"

She thought it was very funny. She glowed like a Christmas tree. Then she said, "I want you to meet Pete."

Pete also stepped into the apartment. He resembled Kelly. They might have been identical twins if she had been a few years older and had a mustache and thickish eyeglasses and, of course, had been a man. And if her toast-brown eyes had been blue.

"From Woods Hole?" I asked.

"He just flew in tonight," said Kelly. "Big surprise. Nobody dreamed . . ." She was a Christmas tree with bubbling lights.

"I didn't want mother to put on the fatted-calf fuss," Pete said. "The plane didn't get in until eight, and I knew she would wait dinner and so on."

He seemed a nice, affable guy. And a frankly spoken one, too. "It's a business trip for me," he said.

"Yuh," I said, "I heard Bob willed you the place here, all he had . . ."

Well, Pete's blue eyes weren't so frank as his talk.

"I didn't mean *that*," he said. "Bob and I were very close in our college years. We were still a resarch team, in fact. He worked here and I worked there, and we mailed our findings back and forth. We intended to publish our study jointly, as collaborators. In fact, we had reached the point where Bob was leaving Scripps and coming to Woods Hole where we could do the final year's work together."

He was throwing a lot at me in a well-organized, systematic, scientific presentation.

Kelly listened and glowed.

I listened and brooded. "And in case he died, he left you the money to carry on the big study alone?"

"I'm not here about the will," said Pete quietly. "I came out to collect Bob's papers, make sure none of his recent research findings are lost in the shuffle. It's quite all right. I have the Institute's permission, but perhaps you had better *check* on that."

"Not what I wanted to check."

Pete's magnified blue eyes looked at me. "I know," he said. "Nothing to it."

"How do you know?" I said.

"I understand what you mean, and there's nothing to it. Nelda told me about you and asked the same question. . . ."

"Nelda!" said Kelly. The Christmas-tree-light effect seemed to have suffered a short circuit.

"She met me at the airport."

"*She* knew you were coming?" said Kelly.

"She phoned me long-distance when Bob drowned. They had to know whether I had ever witnessed a will, or if I knew of one, and to save the telephone bills I told her I was coming out."

I studied Kelly. The lights were struggling to glow again. Brother Pete had explained everything, and why should she doubt?

"Kelly," I said, "do you mind if I speak with Pete alone in the kitchen a minute?"

She minded: "I'm not seventeen any more. Bob meant as much to me as any of you. So count me in."

Pete nodded. "She's right, Svederup. Count her in."

Well, majority rules.

"Nelda told me," said Pete, "of a rumor linking Bob's name with a Dottie Vonn who attempted suicide here in July, '50. I assured her there was nothing to it. Bob at the time was in love with my sister, and even though she did not feel exactly that way about him, he would never have involved himself in any relationship with the Vonn woman."

"He gave blood," I said.

"He was a professional blood donor," said Pete coldly.

"She didn't pay him."

"She didn't pay Dr. Sporwell, who was the physician, either. Doctors don't let patients die because they can't pay, and biology students don't let lives be lost because of the money part. Bob didn't mess around with Dottie Vonn afterward any more than Sporwell did. I told Nelda so, and I tell you so."

Pete could have got into Congress running on this issue. Anyway, he would have had Kelly's vote. I wasn't so satisfied.

"I'd still like a word in the kitchen," I said. "Tell you how Bob died, not pleasant to hear."

Pete followed into the kitchen. I closed the door.

"You a scuba fan?" I said.

"Some."

"Good at it?"

"Fair."

"Honest, not modest."

"I've shot around thirty thousand feet of underwater 16-millimeter."

A photography expert. I would have liked his opinion of the snapshot. It was salt-water-soaked shreds now, along with the rest.

Anyway, I described the sea-floor scene, illustrating the cave formation by steepling my hands.

"Trapped in there," I said, "would you have stripped off your weight belt?"

"God, no."

"Why not?"

"Effect of buoyancy might wedge a person up in that crevice."

"Bob seemed to have forgot that."

Pete's eyes, big behind the thickish glasses, were solemn with deliberate, analytic thoughts. "But Steve was there to help him."

"Steve was *not* there to help him." I told how Steve said he'd gone ashore, then changed that so little Brad wouldn't feel responsible.

Pete pondered. "Well, it needs looking into."

I came closer. He would have to forgive the onions and the liniment.

"*Was* Bob a father?" I demanded.

"No," said Kelly's brother. "Of course not. *Nothing* to that gossip."

I heard or imagined I heard a hedge in his voice.

"Bob's dead. He can't tell me. You have to, Pete."

"Well, he wasn't *really*."

The hedge was there, in plain sight, an accent hung on it.

How to break through?

"Is there such a thing as *un*really?" I said.

His big, glassed-in eyes worried. His face knotted with reticences. He said slowly, tentatively: "As you know, Bob was a blood donor."

It never happened *that* way.

"Well," said Pete, proceeding now in an unorganized, unsystematic, unhappy fashion, "Bob came home with me the next Christmas and New Year's. We hitchhiked. We were strapped financially —oh, we both had part-time jobs, but the next semester coming up meant lab fees we had to scrape together."

"This was still '50?"

"Christmas, '50, New Year's, '51," said Pete. "*After* New Year's, well, that doctor I mentioned came to the rescue."

"How?"

"Why, instead of being a blood donor, Bob had the chance to make a sperm donation."

There it fell, all in a nutshell. In fact, in a bombshell. A dud bomb, Pete must have concluded from my numb-and-dumb expression.

"You've heard of artificial insemination, surely," said he.

Heard of it? I could have told him the dairy farmers around Milquevais hardly ever have a bull in the herd nowadays; the vet comes around with his kit . . . But I decided to leave Milquevais out of the discussion.

"I'd have hesitated, myself," said Pete. "Of course, Bob had that family background to influence him. Parents were people, children were other and distinct people. The blood relationship in itself meant nothing. A natural parent could be a tyrant without any claim upon a child's affection. Decent, generous human beings could be *good* parents without any blood relationship existing. I rather feel Bob acted on these theories as a kind of scientific demonstration. Anyway, he made the donation."

"Did he donate a boy or a girl?" I said.

"He never knew," said Pete, shocked. "They never tell a donor, and there may not have been *any* result."

"If he never knew, what did the scientific demonstration prove?"

"Nothing," said Pete, "except that in a sense, it's possible Bob could have been a father."

NINETEEN

"A PERSON could ask this Dr. Sporwell, but do you think I should?" My eyes questioned Ava Gage.

Outside the Surf Club apartment windows, the waves mewed wetly and sadly on the sands. The tide was out and ebbing.

Inside the apartment, the little rice-paper-shaded lamps glowed on the Japanese prints and African masks and Swedish glass. There was a feeling of far-off and long-gone hands shaping these things and embroidering Ava's dark-green and gold lounging robe that came from a Ceylonese temple. She had her red Titian hair loosened and brushed down onto the brocaded shoulders.

We were alone, with Brad asleep and Steve again off someplace. I'd arrived as Ava was switching off a TV globe-trotting series channeled out of Los Angeles between eleven and eleven-thirty.

She'd offered me a cigarette from a sandalwood box given to her by an appreciative travel agency client. She told me about that, and about the Japanese prints that a museum would have been glad to own and that had been exhibited at the local Art Center. She told me about the Art Center, to which her father had contributed *his* collection of Central American pottery. I said Brad must be a wonderful kid if he could be trusted not to wreck all these art treasures.

"Brad is," she said. "He's always been marvelously responsible, marvelously mature."

"How do you get a kid like that?" I said.

Well, it was a hell of a way to bring up the subject of artificial insemination, but the subject wasn't going to bring itself up, and I had to extend my remarks along the lines of inherited character traits, genetics, and the possibility of a future race of eugenically certified kids like Brad. It might make a magazine article if I could dig up some first-hand human-interest personal-experience data.

"I doubt whether Sporwell or any physician would furnish you with any personal data," Ava said. "You'd run into medical ethics, Ken. I doubt if a doctor could be compelled, even in court, to testify he had performed such a test-tube operation for a woman patient."

"Or impatient woman?" I said.

She considered me with a sober, steady, not unkind look.

"This isn't like you, Ken," she said. "At least, I had thought of you as more of the Huck Finn type."

"I guess if Huck were around nowadays, he'd take to sex as to a corncob pipe."

"Exactly. He'd treat it naturally, and not make embarrassed wisecracks," said Ava, "even with an older married woman in her apartment at this hour of night."

Her manner stayed sympathetic and understanding, making me feel even more of a heel.

"Well, I drove myself to it," I admitted.

"Why did you, Ken?"

"This Huck is on a raft headed for the rocks, Mrs. Gage. There's going to be a rush for the lifeboats, and I don't want to trample any poor innocent kids and women in the dark."

The ocean played the soft sad music on the beach under the apartment windows.

"You mean well, I'm sure," said Ava, "but you don't begin to understand. . . ."

"I'm trying to learn. Going to night school right now."

"Taking the wrong course, though."

"Just so I find the right teacher."

She thought a while.

"It isn't a question of sexy biological details," Ava said then. "The women involved aren't impatient for the reasons you perhaps think. As I understand it, physicians rarely ever resort to this method except in the cases of couples who have been married for years, are getting along into their thirties, and for one reason or another are unable to adopt a baby. Because of age and other factors, the caseworkers prefer placing children in another type of home. And, a black market adoption could lead to all sorts of trouble." She broke off and thought to herself some more.

I knew the kind of trouble she meant. Liz Patterson had it.

"Anyway," said Ava, "the husband and wife are both normal, both pass all the tests, both appear physiologically normal. The usual thing is to try artificial insemination with the husband as the donor. If that fails, then they may resort to an outside donor. Generally one doctor makes that arrangement with a healthy young medical student having the husband's general physical characteristics, and another doctor performs the actual insemination procedure, so the parties involved never meet and can never be known to each other. And absolutely nothing can ever be traced."

Ava was now moving around the room, a slow step at a time, and it seemed to me in rhythm with the sea music outside.

"It might be traced," I said. "The student could count nine months from around New Year's, '51, and there couldn't be so many babies born in early October to mothers having a first child after years of marriage."

She looked at me tiredly. But not fearfully. "It wouldn't be legal proof. The child would be the legitimate child of the legally wedded couple involved."

There was more than law to it. The human side.

"You seem to understand all the aspects of this," I said. "Now, if I asked Steve the same questions, would I get the same answers?"

That's the kind of questions the lawyers ask, probably because that kind of question pulls an answer.

"You mean, did Steve know and consent?" said Ava. "Of course he did, and haven't you seen him with Brad?"

Which let the kitten out of the bag. And a relief it was to us both.

Ava smiled now. "You'd get much more emphatic answers from Steve, because it was more his wish than mine. Because Brad, and the whole family idea, means more to him."

The smile tired a bit.

"I'm not the All-American mother. You must have noticed, Ken. The apartment here, and the office I go to—not that I need be a career woman. We never get very far away from our beginnings, I'm afraid. My father ran a banana plantation, my divorcee mother ran a New York dress shop with dashes to Paris, whereas Steve's dad sold automobiles and his mother darned socks. Steve was the one who saw that having Brad would lend our lives a little of the old-fashioned balance."

A few more, sea-timed steps.

"Didn't you ever wonder, though?" I said.

Ava hugged herself in the Ceylonese temple robe. "I won't lie," she said. "Brad's such a sweet, marvelous, talented, really mature little boy. Yes, I sometimes wondered where he got it, and what his real father was like."

I thought a while by myself. Could Ava have gone overboard emotionally and fallen in love with the ideal, unknown man?

"Did you know Bob Crossway pretty well?" I said.

"Only as Steve's friend," she said.

I thought a while more. Of men swimming, diving, fishing together. And talking. If Steve or Bob, either one, had ever mentioned the artificial insemination thing, what then?

"Did you know Bob was leaving La Jolla and going to Woods Hole?" I said.

"Yes, he had told Steve to put Casa Luna Vista on the market, but friendship for Miss Kelly's brother Pete explained that. Or, Miss Kelly. Bob may have been a little embarrassed by a friend's sister's hopeless devotion."

Not the way I heard it, which had included a hot-rodder in Kelly's life. But if Ava *had* been in love with Bob Crossway, would she have wanted to admit Kelly was Bob's first and hopeless romance?

I listened to the sea softly, musically sloughing on the sands.

"It could have been," I said, "Bob was embarrassed by being his friend's son's real father."

"Bob never knew . . ."

He had known enough to blurt out to H. H. Crossway that he *was* a father and didn't intend to interfere in any way with the child's life.

"Ava," I said, "I just can't be sure. Bob may have suspected and he may have been leaving La Jolla for good on that account."

She was still shaking her head when Steve walked in on us.

He had a right perhaps to fling us a pained stare. Well, I thought I could square that by walking over and firmly gripping his hand so that he'd gather from the onion and liniment that there could be nothing biologically amiss in our late-hour tete-a-tete.

But he had had no such suspicion. He ignored me. "I've just come from police headquarters, Ava," he said.

The surf outside supplied the sadly musical sound effects.

"But, Steve, dear," said Ava, "why did you?"

As far as I could detect, she seemed entirely and understandingly sympathetic. But then, she was always entirely sympathetic. With me. With Brad. With bearded characters who wasted her time planning trips to Madagascar that could never come off. It seemed to me Steve here was receiving exactly the same sympathetic understand as the rest of us, and no more.

"Because, Ava, dear," said Steve in what tried to be a very controlled voice, "I felt the time had come to tell them everything, the whole damned deal."

Ava took a few of those few steps and helped herself from the sandalwood box. She didn't look to her husband, or to me, either, for a light. She struck her own from a box in a tray fashioned of bronze by other long-ago hands in another far-off land.

Steve veered away, through an inner doorway.

I remained quietly attentive, a night-school student learning a lesson.

Steve came back. He held a glass which appeared to contain whisky with little or no water and no ice.

"I had to, Ava," he said. "Blame Svederup. He's the one who sicked Crossway's attorneys onto the trail."

He looked at me, not angrily.

"But don't feel too bad about it, kid," he said. "A cop named Patterson dug it up ahead of you. His young wife came to Ava and me and was hysterical and went down on her knees and begged our help. She was afraid of losing her adopted child. You can't know what an experience like that is, Svederup."

I knew. I had been through the same myself.

"Why'd Patterson's wife come to *you?*" I asked.

Steve's answer fitted. "Because at one time," he said, "before Brad's birth, Ava and I had considered adopting a child. We had the opportunity of making an arrangement with an unmarried mother-to-be. But we decided against a black market baby deal."

He paused as if hoping Ava would confirm this. She had confirmed it earlier, so her silence didn't matter to me. It bothered Steve, though.

"Patterson had dug that up," he said. "Liz Patterson believed we had investigated and knew the identity of the child's father. She wanted the father's consent because the Pattersons had adopted the same child from its mother."

That part had already been confirmed, also.

"Ava and I knew how we would feel about losing Brad, and we knew how Liz Patterson felt," Steve said, still looking at his wife. "But we had to say no; we couldn't help. But we did promise to keep the matter quiet. And tonight, I had to break the promise. . . ."

I realized Steve was spelling all this out more for Ava's benefit than mine. Though he wanted to convince me he had done the right thing, it might help convince her, too.

She spoke at last, in the smallest of tight, strained voices: "It was *my* promise, too. You might have talked this over with me *before* going to the police."

He was on a spot, all right. He took a hasty swallow from his glass and then explained: "I faced an inevitability. I respected Bob's wishes as long as possible. But now it was inevitably going to come out he gave that ten thousand mortgage money to Dottie Vonn, and *why* . . ."

So you see the spot. Ava would never have agreed to disclosing that, and wild horses would not have dragged it from her—because of Bob's memory more than a promise to Liz Patterson. . . .

"But, look, Steve," I said. "Do you really and honest-to-God believe Bob fathered Dottie's kid?"

He stared. He swallowed, but this time not from the glass.

"Bob? No, no!" said Steve Gage. "*Junior*. Junior Crossway got Dottie pregnant before he went to Korea."

TWENTY

IT'D BEEN twenty-two and a half hours since Dottie's drunk, scared voice came over the phone. Trudging to the parking lot beside the mallard pool, my feet dragged in cadence with the surf's dirge.

Actually, I was beginning to hate the sea music—the whole production, plot, cast, and especially the *deus ex machina* named Ken Svederup.

H. H. Crossway had assigned me to find a living grandchild, flesh of his flesh, bone of his bone. I had tabbed two of them! What was this fact going to do to the two kids?

Gloomily, I ground the starter and drove along the hummocked Club pavement.

Brad and Sonny were equally the President and Founder's descendants, on the blood and bones and genes basis. Morally, each was entitled to equal shares in the five million dollar inheritance sweepstakes. Legally, neither the test-tube child nor the illegitimate and subsequently adopted one had a claim. It all depended on what His Highness decided.

I turned the wagon villageward on Torrey Pines Road.

What would His Highness decide?

He might go for Sonny, because Sonny was Junior's son. It would be the sentimental choice. However, the tycoon desired more than a grandchild lisping at his knee. He wanted a successor capable of governing the Crossway newspaper empire. And Sonny was also Dottie's son, with possible genetic tendencies to alcoholism and manic-depressive moods. In fact, all that I could see in Sonny at first glance was the thumb in his mouth.

Therefore, the millionaire might go for Brad. Brad was Bob's son, and Bob had been brighter than Junior, I guessed. Brad was also Ava's son, liberally endowed with genetic superiority on that side. Indeed, anyone's first glance could see Brad's high-octane intelligence and personality quotients.

So which would the old boy take, if he had his choice?

The wagon chugged through the placid shopping district, peaceful at one A.M. as a Milquevais schoolroom during summer vacation.

Of course, Mr. Crossway's was only the first choice. It would hinge next upon how the Pattersons and the Gages responded.

Liz I felt sure of; Ava—I didn't know. Not for the money, anyway—that she clearly had. Still, she might consent to a quiet acknowledgment that Brad *was* Bob's son. The Crossway lawyers would know how to arrange an adoption under which little Brad would attend a fine private school and be on friendly terms with his mother while being slowly acclimatized to the idea of a wealthy grandfather. *If* Ava already thought of him as Bob's son really, and if the prospect of a newspaper empire for the kid appealed to her on the career side. Anyway, Ava I was less sure of than Liz.

As for Steve, how much of the fast-buck influence he bumped into every day had rubbed off on him? And as for Pat Patterson, I already had a thousand dollar bet down that *he* could be had.

I braked at Casa Luna Vista, shut off the motor, and heard the surf again.

There was no camp-trailer truck in sight, and no Pat on the doorstep, and no note in the letter box or under the door.

It'd been twenty-two and a half hours, but I trudged back to the wagon and listened to the surf music a while.

Pat, I decided, would go for it. Liz, I knew, wouldn't. There would be a hell of a family row; Sonny would suffer; and in the end there'd be a stalemate.

Then H. H. Crossway would fix his sights on Brad, and after that I couldn't guess. . . .

Possibly Ava and Steve would stand shoulder to shoulder and repulse the invader. On the other hand, it seemed to me Ava had pretty clearly hinted that the marriage wasn't on the good old-fashioned balance until Brad came along. Ava's parents had been divorced, and it's hard to get away from your beginnings.

Steve and Ava might get a divorce. One of them might die.

After nearly twenty-three hours, you begin to dream with your eyes open. I dreamed that Steve might die, and in this dream Ava wedded herself to H. H. Crossway. Then I dreamed that Ava might die, and Steve was Brad's legal father but knew he wasn't blood and bone relation at all.

At that point I woke up, and ground the starter, and headed toward Claremont. It had just occurred to me that I had the first choice here.

I could give His Highness a line, say nothing about Brad, play a dirty trick on Liz. Technically, the story she told me had been untrue. She had said nothing about Junior being Sonny's natural father.

Or I could name Brad, because technically I had been instructed to trace *Bob's* child. Not Junior's.

Maybe I could save one or the other.

After twenty-three hours you can get to thinking of five million bucks as a plague to be shunned.

It depended, of course, on how far O'Quill and Lowden investigated Steve's statements tonight. They might not investigate them too far. Bob's death was officially an accidental drowning; Dottie's was officially a suicide, and their child was supposed to be dead, too. So what if one party had paid the other a sum of money all of four years ago?

Pat Patterson worried me more. I had to find out about *him*.

Pat's garage door was up, and his camp-trailer truck stood inside. I swung into his driveway, and the wagon's headlights spilled in past the truck body, and I saw Pat. He'd apparently just got home. He was at his garage's rear end, and on his feet, seeming to stare at me.

I reached around into the wagon's rear, fumbled among the scuba gear, and grabbed the heavily weighted diving belt. With that in hand, I went to meet him.

I was inside the garage before I noticed the spear shaft sticking out of his throat.

Somebody had lifted one of the arbalete guns from the garage wall. Those things go off with the force of a high-power big-game rifle. This spearhead had pushed clear through the back of Pat's neck and passed on into the garage boarding behind him. And all so quietly that Liz in the house had heard nothing—she said later.

But I didn't call Liz out now and ask her. Instead I went through the dead cop's pockets. There were no hundred dollar bills on him.

After twenty-three hours, it all seemed kind of dreamlike, a continuation of my earlier bad dreams.

I got back into the wagon and drove out of Claremont down to Highway 101, where I fed a dime into an all-night gas station phone and called headquarters.

A choice faced me. I could return to Pat's garage and wait there for O'Quill and Lowden. Or I could go to Bob's apartment and wait for a prowl-car detail to haul me in to headquarters.

Well, I was too tired to decide. And much too tired to try to save any of the pieces from O'Quill and Lowden. A few hours in that homicide squad office, and I would give them Sonny and Brad and everything else.

So I headed north on 101. At the canyon top stoplight, I turned off onto the Miramar Road, and after a few miles pulled off that onto a smaller road across the mesa, and off that behind a clump of greasewood brush. There I crawled into the back of the Chevie, lay down on the air mattress, and thought a while about Pat Patterson.

He had been digging around and running to everybody, and he had finally dug up something that killed him. And I had been digging around and running to the same people, and maybe it would kill me before I got it dug up.

The night was full of mosquitoes making noises like buzz saws, but finally I fell asleep and slept as well as I could have at Chaparral House. At least, out here nobody knew where to hunt and harpoon *me*.

At least, too, I woke up alive, with the morning sunlight trying to burn the dew drizzle off the wagon's glass.

My thinking started right where it'd left off, with the idea I might be the next victim—*would* be, if there was to be another victim. *Unless* I got in there first with the harpoon.

I even kind of came to like the idea. It had a magnetic quality, one that pulled the scattered particles into a pattern. I even began to feel again like the Courthouse Kid paddling out across Lake Milquevais toward Canadian Jones on his island.

Pushing the idea before me, I drove back into La Jolla, this time by the scenic old Scripps grade along the cliffs. It was farther, but there might be cops looking for a Minnesota-plated station wagon.

From the same reasoning, I detoured onto the hillside streets above Torrey Pines Road. It all came out the same, down near the high school where the Kellys lived.

Kelly and Pete were being served a back-porch breakfast by their mother. Kelly looked glamorous in percale and white cuffs; Pete looked cool in the big glasses and a seersucker suit. Mrs. Kelly looked competent in an apron. I looked like the night-after-sleeping-in-street-clothes with no shave and no breakfast.

Mrs. Kelly rushed inside to put on more coffee and fry me an egg.

"Bob must have felt more at home here than he ever did up on the hill," I said.

The morning paper lay across the breakfast table. I played the scopophiliac and saw Officer Patterson's death all over the front page. The paper said the police were dragnetting for a mystery man who had telephoned about the killing. No allusion to a Minnesota station wagon, though.

"Aunt Debby did her best," Pete was saying. "She lived under Crossway Senior's thumb, and the bravest thing she ever did in her life was will the Casa Luna Vista to Bob. . . ."

And Bob had willed it to *him*. I think Pete expected me to jump him about that again, but I fooled him.

I asked, "What was *Junior* like?"

"I thought everyone knew," said Pete. "Junior was a public figure, a rising financier and young statesman."

"What did Bob think of him, though?"

"I couldn't say. Junior being so much older and living in Chicago, I don't think Bob knew him except as a public figure."

"Pete!" said Kelly. "You knew perfectly well Bob *pitied* Junior."

I looked at Kelly. Her toast-brown eyes flashed with frank disclosures.

"Bob saw Junior *often*," said Kelly. "Junior kept dashing out from Chicago, every month or so, and stayed for a week at a time."

"At the old man's beck and call?" I asked.

"Worse than that. Junior didn't wait to be called. He had learned to lean on his dominating father as on a crutch. That's why Bob pitied him. Moreover," said Kelly, "Bob felt an odd sense of gratitude. Junior acted as his lightning rod, diverting the parental thunder and lightning. As long as Junior lived, Bob was allowed to go his own quiet rebel's way. . . ."

You learn a lot on a back porch. "Didn't Junior ever rebel?" I asked.

"Once," said Kelly. "He married Nelda without asking his father's advice. Bob had high hopes that marriage might make a two-fisted he-man of his big brother. Instead Nelda ganged up with old Mr. Crossway, and they both ran Junior's life for him."

I had the feeling of coming around a corner onto something.

"Maybe Junior rebelled against them both," I suggested, "with another woman."

In Kelly's brown eyes, I drew a blank: she wouldn't know about anything like that. In Pete's blue eyes I drew another blank; if he knew, he wasn't telling.

Mrs. Kelly came out with my egg. She had browned potatoes and made more toast. The toast was of home-baked bread. "Don't let me stop you from talking," she said, poured me a cup of coffee that smelled better than Del Bolling's special blend. Then she poured herself a cup also. "I heard it all," she said, sitting down, "and I might add a thing or so myself."

Why'd she give me such a start? I'd known all along that the women like her back home don't spend all their lives shelling peas and baking bread. They put in some time back-fence gossiping, too.

What Mrs. Kelly had to relate wasn't back-fence gossip, though.

"The summer Bob lived here with us," she said, "and the night the Vonn girl tried to kill herself, a woman phoned earlier and wanted to talk to Bob."

"A drunk, scared woman?" I asked.

Mrs. Kelly nodded.

"Why, mother," said Kelly, wide-eyed, "you never mentioned this before. . . ."

"It was Bob's affair. I felt if there was anything he should tell *us*, he would do it without my questioning him."

I could see where it must have taxed Mrs. Kelly. She must have known Bob was in love with her seventeen-year-old daughter at the time.

"And," said Mrs. Kelly, "later on Bob *did* tell me. He came down after college let out in the spring of '53. He had been in touch with the Vonn girl again. She had a little boy, and one that looked so much like a Crossway that Bob believed it was Junior's child."

Here I'd been seeking the local Florrie Schultz. I had picked the wrong Kelly—that was all.

"Miss Vonn wanted money, and he had given her some."

"How much?" I interrupted.

"I don't know, but, 'Bob,' I told him, 'don't be a fool. Don't give her any more,'" said Mrs. Kelly. She went on:

" 'I can't let my brother's child starve or go on relief,' Bob told me.

" 'Bob,' I told him, 'any money you give *her* won't help that little boy a bit.' And I thought a while. 'You get that girl to place the child in a good foster home,' I said. 'You pay the foster home, and you'll be sure the little boy is getting proper care.' "

And she had kept her mouth shut ever since because it was Bob's personal affair. You know, some of those back-porch ladies make pretty fair mothers-in-law. They aren't the bossing, butting-in, interfering kind.

"But *now*," said Mrs. Kelly, "we must find the child, where-ever it is."

"Don't worry, mother," said Pete, blinking behind his big glasses. "I know where the kid is. Bob made that will with the understanding I would continue the foster home arrangement if anything happened to him."

Well, I guess Bob told a little here, a little there, but not very much to anybody.

But Pete knew about the Pattersons; he had read the morning paper. My eyes quizzed him.

"I promised to keep it a secret," Pete said. "Bob didn't want his father to ever find out. He felt that the old man's domination had messed up Junior's life horribly. Bob had fought the same domination himself, and he didn't want the child to fall a victim to the same influence."

It seemed understandable. I would not have wanted H. H. Crossway's saddle on my back and his bit in my mouth.

"Did Bob pay Dottie ten thousand dollars to keep her from going to Crossway Senior?" I asked.

"I don't know," Pete said. "I think Nelda had frightened Dottie off from trying anything like that, anyway."

"Steve Gage says Bob bought her off."

"Steve! . . . The whole town seems to be in on the secret," Pete said.

"Yuh," I said. "The only privacy a couple of men can get would be out on a tube in the ocean. Or under the ocean. And I think I could borrow Steve's scuba outfit for you, if the idea appeals," and my hands built a steeple over my plate.

"I can borrow gear at the Institute," Pete said.

"I don't mind asking Steve."

"He doesn't have an underwater camera," Pete said. "And I've arranged for the Institute's."

"Want me to show you the place?"

"I know the area fairly well," said Pete, building his hands into a steeple over *his* plate.

"Any particular time in mind?"

"This forenoon. I have to fly back after the services."

"I might sound out Steve and be along later," I said. "But good hunting."

It all annoyed Kelly. "Since when do we say grace after meals?" she puzzled at our hands. "What are you two being so overly subtle about, anyway?"

Mrs. Kelly looked firmly at her daughter. "It's their business, whatever they're up to," she said. "We womenfolk have to learn to trust our menfolk."

I blushed to remember I had once thought Ava the woman-liest of her sex. I'd been a yokel at the circus, after all. The realization sent me to the Kelly phone to tell Nelda, the beautiful bare-back rider, I was on my way up the hill. I told her straight-out, too —no hedging.

TWENTY-ONE

THE PLAIN-FACED, white-aproned maid guided me through the chateau to the upper-crust equivalent of a back porch. This was a basket-weave-walled patio with tinted plastic roofing, fuschias in hanging baskets, fernery in the corners, and a potted exotic plant nested under the glass-topped table where Nelda sat to breakfast.

The rich read the same newspapers we do, and Nelda sat scanning her copy of the front page between exhalations from an ebony and silver cigarette holder. She was a composition in graceful curves inside a morning negligee costume of a cobweb peignoir drawn over something gossamer.

She was scared all over again, right back into her vampire role. Maybe she hoped to seduce the homicide squad.

I greeted her. "You knew it was Dottie and Junior's kid all the time . . ."

"I deny that. None of this concerns me in the slightest degree." She was trying again to bluff me into thinking her dead man's hand of cards ranked above a royal flush. "Svederup, you make any such accusation against me, and I'll prosecute for libel and slander."

"I don't know about juries out here, but back in Milquevais you wouldn't get far with it . . ."

"Back in Milquevais is where you belong," said Nelda loftily, "and it was a mistake you ever left there."

"You're aware how that mistake happened," I said. "Father Crossway was searching for an illegitimate child of whose existence you had known since before its birth."

Nelda merely smiled.

"And it's all going to come out now," I said. "A cop has been killed, and the police will not shrug this one off as accident or suicide. You deny you knew about Junior's kid, Nelda, and they will cram the lie down your lovely gullet."

Her fright increased. So did her pose of imperious disdain. "You explain yourself to the police," she said, "and I'll explain me. But not to you."

"They will grab me first, Nelda. On my answers will depend the questions you get in your turn."

The odalisque eyes blinked. If she satisfied me, would I shut my big mouth about Junior's kid? What could she lose by trying?

"I didn't *know*," said she. "It's true Dottie Vonn came to me in

the summer of '50. She professed to be pregnant, and she blamed
it on Junior. She wanted money. So I took her for a cheap adven-
turess who'd read of my husband's death and imagined she could
cash in on my grief and dread of scandal."

If I knew Nelda, that's just how she would have seen Dottie.
And if I had known Dottie, she had been simply (or com-
plicatedly) a more or less promiscuous, more than less neurotic,
alcohol victim—and no match for Miss Stenographer of 1948.

"I suppose you insulted Dottie, slapped her down with threats
of prosecuting her for libel, slander, attempted extortion. . . ."

"I threw her out," said Nelda grimly. "Another slicker called on
me with a necklace of phony pearls he claimed Junior had ordered
as a gift for me, paying five hundred down and leaving a fifteen
hundred balance for me to pay. I threw him out, too."

I forgot her pearl salesman. He hadn't killed Bob, Dottie, and
Patterson. He wasn't lying around the next corner to kill me,
either.

"One night later, Dottie phoned you . . ."

Nelda betrayed annoyance. "How do you know all this?"

I knew Dottie had phoned Bob; calling Nelda was logical, too.
"I have my sources."

The Oriental eyes narrowed, perhaps trying to read my mind.
I narrowed my eyes right back at hers.

She shrugged. "Dottie did call me one night and say she was
committing suicide and leaving a note blaming Junior. I still believe
she was faking, trying to hijack me with her threats. She was
drunk, and the razor blade slipped . . ."

"How do you know she used a razor blade?"

"I went to her," said Nelda. "She looked dead in a puddle of
blood in front of the gas stove. I turned off the gas, picked up the
note, phoned for an ambulance, and got out of there."

"Go on."

"That's it. Dottie sobered up and drifted on somewhere else."

"Recently . . ." I said.

Nelda took time out to insert a fresh cigarette into the holder.
It resembled the kind of time-out a quarterback calls to rally his
team on a threatened goal line.

"Look," she said. "It proves I didn't know positively Junior was
her kid's father. You asked, you found out, now beat it."

"You knew positively Bob wasn't the father. What about that?"

Nelda eyed me like a county fair judge sizing up the livestock.
I guess she finally saw I was no 4-H entry.

"I overheard Father Crossway and Robert quarreling rather
loudly in the study one night," she said. "Robert mentioned his
child, and I didn't know but he might be secretly married. He
could marry later on or acknowledge his kid in some way. The
claims of a grandchild might make plenty of trouble in probate
court one day."

I was reminded of her anxiety about Bob's dying words and oral or written will. And of her relief when Bob's will named only Pete Kelly.

Nelda continued. "Besides, Junior was the oldest and Father Crossway's favorite. So if there had to be *any* grandchild, Junior's kid ought to come first. I decided to look up Dottie and investigate her story."

All for Junior's kid's sake, of course. I did not laugh aloud. I said, "You've had over a month to do that."

"I had to find Dottie, and it wasn't so easy."

"How did you find her?"

"Well, I knew Del Bolling. Del knew Patterson."

I could not help frowning.

"Del knows about everybody," said Nelda.

He did. And Del multiplied the cast and thickened the plot. I did not want to miss any of it. You listen good when your life hangs on getting the details straight.

"Del said Patterson, being a cop, could look into the police bureau records. Dottie might have a record. Anyway, Patterson did locate Dottie in Las Vegas. Del brought her down here with promises of getting her onto her feet and into a job."

"So?"

"So Dottie said the child was hers and *Robert's,* and she said it was dead, anyway."

"Did she call him Robert?"

"Bob."

"Suppose *you* call him Bob," I said. "Why did she say it was Bob's child and dead?"

"Dottie didn't like me enough to do me any favors," said Nelda pointedly.

I shook my head. It was true as far as it went, but it didn't go far enough.

"Maybe she was bought off," Nelda offered.

"Who would buy her off?"

"Bob was alive then. He may have paid her. Bob wasn't doing me any favors, either."

I shook my head.

"Del might have bought her off himself," Nelda said next.

"Why would Del?"

"I never told Del the whole truth," Nelda said. "As far as he knew, Bob *was* the father. He may have paid Dottie to say the kid was dead and kept the secret of the living child for leverage on me. You said so yourself last night."

Last night Patterson had been alive. Last night I had not known Junior was the father. I would have shaken my head, but Nelda shook hers first.

"Maybe Patterson *scared* Dottie off," she said.

"Why would he?" I asked.

"Because Liz and Pat Patterson had the kid themselves." Nelda gave me her Oriental look. "I bet you never knew *that*."

I play-acted no pretended surprise. "How did you know it?"

"Pat told me," said Nelda.

I play-acted to cover up surprise.

"Sure," said Nelda. "Pat and Bob both belonged to the skin diver crowd. Bob knew the Pattersons wanted a child. At that time, anyway, Pat was a clean-cut young cop. So Bob arranged for the Pattersons to take Sonny as a foster child. Pretty soon Liz wanted to adopt the kid outright, and that's when Pat stopped being so clean-cut."

"It's legal to adopt a child," I said. "*Why* would Patterson scare Dottie, make her say the kid was dead?"

Nelda forgot the fancy holder and stuck a fresh cigarette into the corner of her mouth.

"Nobody told Bob of the adoption," she said. "Pat went right on collecting the foster care payments from Bob as before."

"Did Pat tell you that?"

"I figured it out."

"How?"

"Well, that's the point."

So we had come to the point. And high time.

Nelda had forgotten to light her cigarette. It bobbed with her lip movements.

"Pat was like everybody else," she said. "He thought all along Bob was Sonny's father. He figured Bob just didn't want to admit it. And for a while, Pat was only in this thing trying to keep Sonny for Liz, and trying to cover up the foster-care pay angle."

"After a while?" I said.

"After a while," said Nelda, "he dug up more. Enough to give him bigger ideas."

Enough to stand him up against a garage wall with an arbalete spear through his throat.

"Come to that point," I said.

"The adoption probably wasn't worth a damn," said Nelda. "Because the natural father never signed his consent, and because Pat could testify Dottie was dead drunk when she signed her consent. It could have been annulled, and I could have adopted Sonny myself."

I stared. I could see her doing it. Bringing Junior's kid into the chateau as *her* adopted child. Making her the queen-mother of the honey hive, and her the one to give H. H. Crossway a flesh and blood heir.

"You mean," I said, "you propositioned Patterson to testify the adoption was fraudulent?"

What was I yakking about? Nelda viewed me wonderingly.

"Why not? Who'd more right to Junior's kid than Junior's widow?"

That's how she characteristically saw it.

I thought of Liz mothering Sonny, nursing him through measles, mumps, and whooping cough, putting the fairy's dime under the pillow in exchange for the lost milk tooth, baking the birthday cakes, kissing the bumped places, *loving* her adopted baby.

Nelda, naturally, had never given Liz Patterson a thought.

"Did Pat agree to that?" I demanded.

"We hadn't agreed on the terms. Maybe he'd decided to agree," said Nelda. "Maybe his wife killed him, do you suppose?"

So she had given Liz a thought, after all.

TWENTY-TWO

I DROVE down the hill, and to be honest about it, somewhere along the way I found myself no longer pushing the idea—the notion that somebody would try to kill me next. It'd got behind and was pushing *me*. Like the fellow back home who tried to fell a chopped tree by pushing at it, and it fell on him.

I'd been relying too much on my cheese-town experience, and what did it amount to?

Canadian Jones was all. Canadian had been a smalltime 'legger, about all the underworld we had in Milquevais. He killed a man for the hip-pocket bankroll, and then he ran for cover. The only mystery had been what cover and how to smoke him out.

Well, I'd come into this deal with the illusion I could easily solve the Crossways' and everybody else's problems—if I took an interest and cared to. And if somebody put it up to me in a light that aroused my sympathy.

In fact, I'd figured I could find out who was in the right and then blow the whistle so that the right parties would come out unhurt. All because I took for granted that crimes are committed by criminals—with or without police records, but anyway by criminals who had been cutting corners a long time. Very simple. Follow the cut corners, and around one of them I was bound to find the guilty person, forced to jump me to conceal the secret. Well, it wasn't that simple.

I drove down into the picturesque, eucalyptus- and palm-frond-shaded village, and I couldn't see anything but cut corners and people hugging secrets. From low tide to hilltop and clear on over to Claremont, it seemed the same. From San Diego harbor to Las Vegas, it was the same. Dottie with her illegitimate child, Liz with her adopted Sonny, Ava with her test-tube Brad, even Mrs.

Kelly with her grown-up son and daughter, carried locked bosom secrets. The men, likewise. The dead cop, old Crossway playing me for a cat's-paw, Bob Crossway hiding the identity of his brother's son, Del Bolling on his cabin cruiser—all cut corners. In fact, if you asked the homicide squad, Ken Svederup had covered up more secrets and cut more corners than anybody else.

So what did it prove?

Well, for a wonder, this morning I found Steve Gage in his office. He looked full of secrets and treacheries, too. It could have been the effect of the little water and no ice last night.

"Well, Steve, I just stopped by to see if you'll go on the record now with what you told me in the Club bar the night Bob died."

A sober moment followed. "Couldn't you be building this up subconsciously?" said Steve. "Ava says *you* delayed Brad past five o'clock. You might be crying murder to clear yourself of the responsibility for the accident. Subconsciously."

Well, I hadn't expected he would go along with it. "At least," I said, "I'm not crying accident and clearing somebody of the responsibility for murder."

That made no impression, either.

"Anyway, Pete Kelly and I are having a look down there," I said.

"You're wrong," said Steve, "but I'll come along with you and Pete."

"You don't have to."

"The dip will do my head good."

He pushed some soybean market reports off his desk top into a drawer. It reminded me of a fellow back in Milquevais who lost his shirt gambling in grain futures. Some have to lose so the Del Bollings can win. Steve considered Del a friend, so I kept the thought to myself.

Steve's Cadillac led the way out Torrey Pines Road and the Shores Road, leaving it to the other motorists to save the fenders. By the time I parked, he was waiting in the shanty Brad had visited that night.

I toted my stuff in from the station wagon. His was already hung up on the wall of this outbuilding, along with other gear and other items of marine equipment needing repair. It seemed to be a kind of tool shed.

"Want to wait for Pete?" Steve asked.

"We could go ahead and find the place," I said. "I thought you wore your wetsuit home the other night."

"I was out the next day with a police department diver," said Steve.

That cleared up one reason he'd been hard to find.

We changed. I donned trunks and wetsuit, and as I buckled on the weight belt, I said, "What's the police diver make of Bob's belt down there in that hole?"

"I shoved it in there," Steve said. "I had to get it off Bob to raise him to the surface."

That cleared *that* up.

Steve helped me with the lung. It was a back-pack compressed-air cylinder with the pressure gauge needle pointing to full, and with twin air tubes that came around the wearer's neck to a mouth-plug piece.

"You know about these things?" I said.

"Bob and I traded off," he said. "Changed back and forth."

Steve wasn't wearing one, just trunks and shortie shirt and a dagger on his weight belt. We picked up fins and masks and snorkels and a tire with a line on it.

"We don't want an arbalete along?" he asked.

"I don't intend to shoot anything," I said. "Do you?"

"Go, then."

We plodded down to the beach beyond the pier to where Bob's body had lain on the sand. The sand was heavily tracked up. If anyone had gone off the rocks ahead of us into the water, there was no sign of it. The water looked cold and gray and rather deadly.

We rinsed the masks and went in, Steve handling the tire and steering it upright in front of him through the water. He stopped after a while, let down the tube between us, and looked at me through his face-plate. He removed the snorkel tube from his mouth to speak.

"Here we are."

I removed my snorkel and pushed up my mask. "You sure?"

"Within a few feet."

"You have it lined up good," I said.

"I lined it up for the police diver."

We watched each other across the tube.

"Incidentally, the guy took all of Bob's stuff up from the bottom," said Steve. "What did you hope to show Pete, anyway?"

I told him: "Say a man pulled one of these weights out of his belt. Say he socked the other guy smack on the face-glass. I assume the blow could knock the victim unconscious, and yet the mask rubber would prevent any bruises."

A swell lifted and dropped the tube. In spite of the wetsuit, I felt chilled.

"It isn't possible to strike an effective blow underwater," Steve said.

"Did you ever try?"

"No," said Steve.

I grinned bravely. Any grin here was a brave one.

"Let's try," I said. "You pull a weight from your belt, and we'll go down. I'll be Bob Crossway with the lung on, and you see whether you can knock me out."

The cold gray sea swells slid by us, and the surf nearly two

hundred yards away played funeral march music. Steve Gage
pushed his mask up onto his forehead and stared at me intently.

"I couldn't do that, Ken," he said. "Great Christ, I might hurt
you."

"You just said yourself it's impossible. . . ."

"No," Steve said, "and if that's what's on your mind, I'm
heading for the beach right now. You can try that stunt with Pete
when he comes, if he's insane as you are."

He pulled down and adjusted his mask.

"I have a few other items in mind," I said hastily.

He frowned behind his plate-glass oval.

"It would have been so easy and simple for anybody to have
gun-speared a fish ahead of time and had it staked out down here
below."

The frown deepened. "That bass was shot with Bob's own arbalete, from off our tube," Steve said.

"Well, those spearheads and lines are a commercial product,
aren't they?"

"Yes . . ."

"Hard to tell what arbalete was used. Anyway, you cut the fish
loose. It got away."

A gull circled overhead and decided there was nothing in us
for him.

"I had to cut the line to float the tube in," Steve said. "Reason I
needed help was I couldn't keep Bob up and do that, too."

"I'm not accusing *you*. I just said the fish could have been staked
out ahead of time."

"Oh," said Steve. "Well, I suppose such a thing might be technically, theoretically feasible."

So I had gained an inch of ground. If you could call it ground,
the nearest terrain being the slab rock thirty to forty feet straight
down.

"How long have divers been known to fight fish?" I said.

"I don't know the world record. Hours, maybe."

"Then this fish could have been shot with another arbalete and
staked out hours ahead. . . ."

The gull came back for another look.

"And, Steve, this is restricted water, not open to the skin diving
crowd. A staked-out fish wouldn't have been noticed."

"Technically. Theoretically."

"The guy would have had to be able to find the place again.
And you have to admit that also is possible, to within a few feet."

The swells rode by, the shore music played its dirge.

"You want me to change my story, Ken? Admit I wasn't out
here with Bob when this thing happened?"

"Just want the truth, Steve."

"The truth could hurt Brad. Psychologically. And for what?
Your guesses *prove* nothing."

He had a good argument there. The sea does not retain finger-prints and footprints to take into court.

Steve had a good grip on the tire, too. His fingers dented into it. My fingers tried. My fingers were cold and numb and fumbled vainly over the slick, slippery surface.

He decided. "I won't hurt Brad for any possible result."

"Murder was possible," I said, fumbling over the slick, slippery surfaces of the whole deal, "if somebody had the motive."

"What motive? Bob had no interests aside from his work, no enemies professionally or personally. Besides being such an ideal-istic, really sweet guy."

"*That* could be a motive," I said. "Women go for the sweet-guy type. It has worried me about Kelly."

"Kelly?" said Steve.

"She seems to have set Bob Crossway up on a pedestal as the all-round example of everything a man should be. Now, say a man married Kelly—that could get tough. It might gravel a husband to have his wife forever and unendingly in her own mind comparing him to an idealized idol. The husband could come to hate the sound and sight of Bob Crossway."

And that went for Steve and Ava Gage, too. It went double for Steve and Ava Gage, because Bob was their child's blood and genes father.

I didn't mention it, though, because this time the gull and an-other gull came around for a swooping look-see. And this trip, I caught onto what attracted the birds.

They'd spotted bubbles breaking the sea surface off past Steve's shoulder.

Birds are sharp-eyed—very. I've known mallards to fly right up to a duck blind where a hunter is waiting, and scare off because they've spotted the guy's rising, frosty breath.

These bubbles came stringing up from below, where Pete Kelly with an underwater lung hunted with an underwater camera.

Had Steve noticed, and was that what made him so cagy? If he hadn't noticed yet, the gulls would soon call the bubbles to his attention. I had to crowd him . . .

"What if it was just the ten thousand dollars?" I said.

"What if? . . ."

"The motive. Say the murderer only cared about the money and didn't give an incidental damn whether Dottie had her baby by which Crossway and all that."

"Theoretical murderer," said Steve restrainedly.

"It wasn't any theoretical ten thousand bucks. You had the power of attorney and you put the second trust mortgage on Bob's building and raised the money, so you know."

Well, nothing around that corner except a blind alley. "I had the power of attorney because Bob was away in school, and I had to act in a zoning matter," said Steve. "Fight off a garish seafood eatery being constructed next door, the kind of thing we are always fighting off in La Jolla. Bob didn't have the time or interest to attend hearings and file protests."

The next corner, though.

"The money. Say the killer cared about that. Nothing more, nothing less."

Of course, I had had to nose around a lot of corners to settle on this one.

"Dottie undoubtedly drank up or gambled away the money long ago," said Steve.

"What if she never got it, though?"

He thought. The thoughts crinkled the eyes inside the oval of his face-plate. The color of his eyes matched the stainless steel rim around the oval glass.

"You're thinking of some man behind Dottie and using her," Steve said. "Del Bolling, is that your idea?"

"You named him. I didn't."

"I named him to show how ridiculous all this is. Del's too *big* . . ."

I shrugged. In a wetsuit and in water a shrug is wasted effort.

"You're trying to explain Dottie's death, actually," said Steve. "You think some hoodlum used Dottie to mulct Bob of ten thousand dollars. Patterson dug into it, and Patterson was a cop. The hoodlum decided Dottie was too alcoholic and too neurotic to hold out under the cop's pressure. With a gun at her back, he forced her to make telephone calls and write a suicide note that she may have thought was a farewell note. Then he marched her out into the water and held her head under. . . . That what you think?"

There were three gulls, now, hovering and watching intently.

Steve watched me just as intently. "It's the same subconscious pattern, Ken. *You* were suspected of killing Dottie. You are trying to turn the girl's suicide into a murder that you can hang on somebody else. To clear yourself of any lingering suspicion. Subconsciously."

"You are well informed about the phone calls," I said.

"Well, damn it, I went to O'Quill and Lowden with the facts about this ten thousand dollars, and we went over all these possibilities."

"I don't think Bob ever gave Dottie any ten thousand dollars," I said. "Not his kid, and why would he?"

"For Junior's child. Bob was depriving the child of recognition as a possible Crossway heir. He may have felt guilty about that. Subconsciously."

I shook my head.

"I think Dottie told the truth when she said Bob helped her

with a few hundred at the time and over the years paid for Sonny's support. That he could easily have done out of his income."

"Aren't you just a little obsessed with all this?"

"Maybe Bob never saw the ten thousand," I said. "Maybe you put it in your pocket or into a fast-buck deal."

I had come to one of those points again.

"Think I'm a *crook?*" asked Steve incredulously.

I had thought all along there was a crooked mind behind and around the cut corners.

"It could be kind of easy to turn crooked," I said, "when you secretly hate a man and want to revenge yourself on him. When your wife admires him excessively, and you don't want to sink in her estimation by asking her for *her* money. When you need the quick cash, and it looks safe. Bob would never have known there was a second trust mortgage against his property, because you managed the business end. Unless he sold the building and then in escrow the trust deed mortgage would show up. If that happened, I think he cared enough about money and disliked sharpshooting phonies enough to have made it tough on you."

A gull dropped down close and was chased away by the next swell.

"You think I killed Bob," said Steve Gage.

I did not apologize and take it all back as being just a subconscious vagary.

"Dottie, too," said Steve.

"Well, with them both dead, you could get away with saying you gave Bob the money and he gave it to her."

"If I had known she even existed," said Steve. "When I took the ten thousand, theoretically."

So I asked, "What was all that about the unmarried girl's baby you decided against adopting before Brad came?"

And he said, "Rather dumb of me to let you meet the girl before I murdered her, wouldn't you agree?"

"It struck me as kind of bright, Steve," I said. "Dottie had taken money of Bob's, and any explanations she offered would have helped your case."

I didn't accuse him of planting the snapshot in Bob's apartment for me to find. Or for the cops to find. I wanted to stick to the point.

He wanted to slide off around it to something else behind another corner. "Well, Ken," he said, "I believe I know what put such suspicions into your mind. It was my failure to recognize Dottie in the Maritime Room. The simple truth is, she had changed over the years and had a different hair-do, and I just did not recall the girl at all."

"Wasn't that."

"What then?"

"Patterson."

"Patterson?" he asked.

"I think your foot slipped, and he had you by the ankle."

Steve said nothing, but he wasted no attention on the gulls.

"I imagine Patterson had you about wrapped up and ready for delivery downtown," I said. "All by himself, to show those headquarters dicks how to do a job. And I further imagine you went downtown and cleared yourself as best you could, and on the way home stopped off in Claremont to kill Patterson."

Steve was shaking his head.

"Yesterday at headquarters," I said, "right in front of the cop, you made that dumb crack about Dottie probably wanting Bob's apartment to put her head into the gas oven . . ."

Steve explained. "I was tired," he said. "It was a tasteless reference to the girl's previous suicide attempt."

"But how'd you know the stove in her Dulcine Street apartment was an electric? . . . If you did not even recall her face at the Maritime Room, you must have been in her apartment later that night."

He smiled. "You're wrong, Ken," he said. "And to prove it, I'm willing to go through with your experiment. In the first place, show you Bob could not have been killed as you think. To make it conclusive, I'll play the victim, and you try to slug me with a weight from your belt."

You see where a guy ends with an idea he pushed around until it begins to push him. ·

"Okay?" said Steve.

"Okay," said I. Because there is no use chasing around all those corners and backing off from the last one. Also because I had sat in that homicide office squad long enough to know how an innocent man feels there. And if Steve was innocent, I didn't want to see him there. It had been circumstantial evidence against me, I remembered.

Steve keeled his face-plate into the sea and rolled on under. I shoved the lung mouthpiece into my teeth, took a hard bite of it, and did the somersault and fin thresh. There must have been more weights on my belt, lending me velocity that slid me past, gliding under and beyond Steve.

The water was a light-green motionless bath that turned bluer and darker and denser in the depths. It felt colder, too, but the wetsuit kept out the cold fine. The pressure started pushing at my ears. I swallowed, and that worked fine.

I'd been holding my breath instinctively. Around twenty feet down, I pushed out the first bubbles and tried hauling a fresh gulp through the mouthpiece. The lung worked fine, too.

Another ten feet, and the rock slabs loomed ahead. I used my hands to push off the nearest, toward a spot underneath the gulls. I hoped. You can get mixed up on directions and distances down there.

I made out the upside-down-V cave mouth a little to the left of where I'd thought it should be.

To keep Steve from peering in there, I came to a stop. The man at the sport shop had demonstrated how easily the weight belt could be jerked off. Hand on the trick buckle, I hoped that would work fine also.

I had lost Steve.

Then a blow fell on the back of my head.

It stunned, blurred things, but it didn't really hurt so much.

Then a hand hooked its fingers into the headstrap of my face mask and twisted. On land it could easily have wrung my neck like a Milquevais chicken's. Down here in the deep, all of me rolled with my twisted head and neck.

Another hand socked onto the mouthpiece tubes of my lung apparatus, and ripped and twisted and fought to break the plug out of my jaws.

I was conscious. I saw the hand, and the body looming as big as a whale, as ugly as a shark. I saw the bared teeth gleaming, and the eyes half-bursting out of the swollen, frantic face behind its oval glass. He didn't look like Steve Gage, or anything else human.

He had it tough, too, just his own lung-power to go on with. So it struck me that probably when it happened the first time, the killer and not Bob Crossway had actually been wearing the lung.

I fought for my life.

The heel of his fin-fitted foot rammed into my belly, socked the wind out of me, and my mouth gaped open for the salt brine to rush in.

I saw black, and my hands stopped fighting him to drop and tear crazily, trying to root his fin out of my belly to get at the so-easily loosened weight-belt buckle.

Somehow I made it, and the black dissolved into blues and greens as the wetsuit's buoyancy brought me up into *air*—I'd got topside, and found myself with a hand pinching the inner tube practically in two, while the shaking legs under me threshed on and on in their automatic, conditioned-reflex kick. I gagged, spat, coughed, between gulps of air.

The water next to me boiled hugely. Pete Kelly surfaced first, his lung cylinder humped over his shoulders, one hand clutching Steve Gage's scuba dagger, the other clutching Steve.

Steve had used up his self-contained breath by the time Pete charged out of the sea cave to tackle him.

We hoisted the unholy specimen onto the inner tube and rushed him ashore.

I had a two-inch scalp gash to show for it. Pete had some nice footage of underwater photography showing the killer trying to drown me.

Steve, it turned out, had a thousand dollars in C-notes in his office safe. The serial numbers matched. He had been going to put that windfall into soybean futures. Where he'd lost the ten thousand dollars mortgage money came to light during the trial.

TWENTY-THREE

A FEW WEEKS later Kelly and I were watching a sunset for the green flash. The green flash occurs when the sun sinks into the sea, ". . . caused by the blue water refracting the reddish rays," Kelly explained.

To see this phenomenon, Kelly had obtained a fresh wave in her toast-colored hair and was wearing the same attractive frock that'd been caught in the convertible hood the first time I ever saw her. I had steered the station wagon into Torrey Pines Park, which is a coastal bluff topped by picturesque, gnarled trees that grow nowhere else in the U. S. A., as Kelly explained.

It was only a short way north of La Jolla, and we arrived early and had the parking place to ourselves.

"Rather a romantic view," said Kelly.

"You ought to see a stand of Minnesota pines," I remarked. "And for that matter you ought to see a Milquevais sunset with the whole sky afire—caused by the refraction from the prairie dust and ragweed pollen."

Kelly changed the subject to the murder trial.

It's the same everywhere. Canadian Jones surprised hardly any of his friends by turning into a killer, and Steve Gage's crimes did not defy belief by the villagers who knew him best, or, anyway, longest.

"Those smashed fenders should have tipped us off," said Kelly. "I've read in a book on abnormal psychology that the ratio of automobile collisions among drivers with criminal tendencies is significantly high."

"Probably the same book which enabled you to spot me as a scopophiliac," I said.

"Well, I know you better now."

However, she changed the subject.

"I imagine Brad will be happier in the long run," she said. "A child can't be exactly comfortable with a father who makes such a show of sacrificial parental nobility. I suspect Brad was becoming old enough to catch onto that act of Steve's."

"It did cloy."

"I wonder what will become of Brad and Sonny finally," she said.

I answered that Ava was more than well-heeled enough to provide Brad with a first-rate education. Pete would use the Casa Luna Vista income to provide equal advantages for Sonny.

"Afterward," I said, "neither should have too much difficulty landing upper-echelon jobs with fine salaries and bonuses in the Crossway newspaper empire."

"If Mr. Crossway lives that long."

"The years fly," I said. "People marry and raise a family before you know it. Mr. Crossway may yet live to see his blood and bone great-grandchildren. If he doesn't, the trustees will know what to do."

"Trustees?"

"The attorneys are putting the Crossway Press, Inc., into one of those trust arrangements," I said. "Mr. Crossway will head it during his lifetime. And he has asked me to serve as a trustee."

Kelly looked at me. Her eyes were bright and admiring. "Why, Ken," she said, "I bet you thought of that solution and sold it to him."

"No salesmanship was needed," I said. "The President and Founder never wished for any grandsons running riot among his roses. He wanted a lineal descendant to take over the helm of state eventually, and I have no doubt that Brad will one day be chairman of the board of trustees unless Sonny wins by a chin."

Kelly continued looking in my direction, only farther off.

"This trusteeship," she said, "might involve your moving to the West Coast?"

"No," I said.

"Oh," she said.

"The pay will be largely nominal, too," I said. "Of course, with it and my Milquevais *Globe* salary, plus selling an occasional book, or magazine article anyway, I should be able to support myself and even a wife and family."

Kelly listened attentively.

"Well, that's it," I said.

However, she refused to change the subject. "What's it like, living in a place like Milquevais?"

"It varies. The summers get hot. One-ten in the shade, strong men falling down of sunstroke, babies breaking out with the heat rash."

"I imagine the falls are nice, though."

"Fall is the hay fever season," I said. "Caused by the ragweed pollen."

"Oh," said Kelly.

"The winter ends the hay fever. The thermometer falls to thirty below, motorists perish in the blizzards, school children get chilblains struggling through the seven-foot snowdrifts."

Kelly looked at me some more. Her eyes darkened to the color of burnt toast.

"All right, Ken," she said. "What's she like?"

"Who?"

"The girl back home," she said. "The one who dotes on the sunstrokes and blizzards and you."

So for the good of all concerned, I made a frank and exact statement.

"Her name is Florrie Schultz," I said. "She is a splendid intellectual young woman of about thirty years of age who works in the public library and corrects my manuscripts, and loves every word I write, including the misspelled ones. At a Platonic distance, I have always admired and even idealized Florrie, just as you admired and idealized Bob Crossway."

Kelly gazed away at the sunset.

"Then if you ever marry, your wife needn't be jealous of Miss Schultz," she said. "Now tell me about the Milquevais white Christmases and husking bees, and the ice-skating and barn dances and all that kind of fun."

So I made a frank and exact statement about that also.

"It's the same as everywhere else," I said. "We have air-conditioning in summer and oil heat in winter. The Christmases are sometimes a muddy gray, and the corn is husked mechanically. We watch the ice carnival and barn dances on TV from the Twin Cities."

Kelly squeezed my arm.

"Oh, Ken," she said. "Look."

The sun slid into the sea, leaving a momentary vivid green wink.

"What?" I said.

"The flash. Didn't you see it?"

"No, I missed it," I said. "We'll have to try another sunset. How about tomorrow night?"

www.ingramcontent.com/pod-product-compliance
Lightning Source LLC
Chambersburg PA
CBHW022034170626
46808CB00003B/1193